Christmas
AT CUMMINGS

Christmas
AT CUMMINGS

BOOK ONE

BRIGITTE CARTER

Christmas at Cummings
Book One

Copyright © 2022 by Brigitte Carter

Book Design by Alt 19 Creative

To all the ones that believed this would be real, even before me and to those who prayed for its fruition especially Mama Carter.

CHAPTER 1

LOUISE MADE ONE last check in the mirror. Her kinky hair was in a tight bun and the only makeup she had on was lipstick, a soft shade of pink that complimented her dark brown skin. She had on her favorite navy suit, tailored perfectly to enhance her curvy body. Practical two-inch block heels advanced her height. She was ready for the day as she grabbed her coffee, her coat, and headed out the door.

Louise didn't have far to go, only a 550-foot walk to the entrance of the Cummings Estate. AND spa, as she liked to correct people. The spa opened two years ago, but it was her crowning achievement so far in adding luxury amenities to the estate that had been in her family for generations. Her home used to be a tool/gardening cottage on the grounds, rebuilding it herself after she graduated college. She didn't want to live in the town near or with her parents; she wanted to be available twenty-four hours a day for the staff at the Cummings.

The Cummings Estate was situated between a mountain and the small town of Sacamore, Pennsylvania. A wealthy family built the Estate in the early 1800s. Louise's family purchased the estate and surrounding land and turned it into a hotel.

As Louise stepped over the threshold, she took a few seconds to admire the spacious hotel. No matter how old she was, the Cummings was a place of joy for her. As a child, she would stand in this spot and look up to the ceiling art to admire her home. It was a cathedral ceiling with wood carvings. The wood was hand carved by her great-great-grandfather and featured intricate designs of flowers and butterflies along the columns, adorned with a cherub at the top of each one. It made her proud to think that they carved her history up there.

Louise enjoys her tradition of taking a few seconds before the day starts. She walks to her office, waving at the bellmen on duty and the front desk clerks. Jamal, her cousin, and assistant manager, greets her in the hall leading to the administrative offices. Jamal is the same shade of brown as Louise and they both share the same wide nose. Other than that, their similarities end. He is tall and lithe, looking like a dancer in another life. He keeps his hair closely shaved to his head. He has a wide, bright smile that greeted her when she saw him.

"You are here early," she remarked, looking at her watch, which said 6:35 a.m.

"Good morning to you too," Jamal said. "I thought you would want to talk before our meeting today."

"The meeting is not until 11. You aren't usually showing your face until after 8. What is the real reason you are here?" Louise inquired.

"Can't the assistant manager make sure everything is perfect for today?" Jamal replied.

Louise rolled her eyes as she opened the door to her office. She felt Jamal had a serious reason for being at the hotel so early, but she was too occupied to press him. Today was the fall board of directors meeting. She needed to focus on her expansion presentation. The expansion she was planning would have them building an additional hotel on the land and create a separate section to build cabins closer to the mountain. It would require the purchase of more land, not to count the millions building the structures. To pay for her plans, she would need to take out an additional mortgage on the hotel. She knew that the additional mortgage would be difficult to get past the board. They were on schedule to get the current mortgage paid off in five years. With this mortgage paid off, they would own the current estate and land out right.

Louise would have to convince the board that the new expansion would set them up for future generations. When finished, it would bring in a staggering amount of revenue, causing them to pay off the new loan in only ten-fifteen years. She knew her plan was great. The other staff also agreed but getting the conservative board to agree to it would be a challenge. It didn't help that the board members were relatives. Some members, like her grandmother, still treated her as a child. Louise could tell her grandmother favored their eldest cousin Malcolm and initially wanted him to take the reins of the estate.

Well, she was the one that was the general manager, so they had to trust her plans. Or at least listen to them. She settled into her desk and Jamal still hovered at her door.

"What is it, Jamal?" she asked. "Do you need some coffee?"

He looked deep in thought. "No, no coffee for me, it's too early."

"Then why are you here?" She said.

"Snippy much? I just wanted to check on you. You were so stressed last night. Why don't you do a spa treatment before the meeting? I can handle things."

"I appreciate that. But sitting and 'relaxing' will be more stressful for me. And anyway, Grandmother will be down for breakfast soon and after yesterday's dinner, I want someone to be there to calm the servers. It would be great if you kept her distracted," she pleaded. "You can talk up the new spa."

"She is the one who needs it," she murmured.

Jamal laughed and sat down. "I would rather clean the pool filter."

"I know," she replied. "But please. I can't handle her this early in the morning. I also need to make sure Chef Henri and his staff have everything perfect for 'Queen Mother'."

"Ok, but I can't understand why you two don't get along. You both are alike—" She looked up, ready to throw her pen at him. "As far as the Cummings is concerned." he said, holding his hands up for protection. She rolled her eyes and put down the pen.

"Well, we both love the Cummings, but have different ideas about how to run it. I want her and the board to understand that I want so much for this estate. It is everything to me."

Jamal reached out and covered her hand. "I know, honey. They will see your vision."

"What about Malcolm?" Louise asked.

This time, Jamal rolled his eyes. "Don't worry about him. You know my brother has his ideas, but we will bring him around. Your parents are on your side, and so is my dad. Mom is on the fence as usual, but she is always trying to please Grandmother. You worry about Uncle Frank and his side. Ultimately, what grandmother says will go." He let go of her hand. "You got this, Weezie."

She smiled at his childhood nickname for her. She knew that worrying anymore couldn't help.

"You are right, Jay. Let me go talk to Chef Henri. We better get on it. Grandmother will be down and ready at seven."

They both headed to their next stop.

After meeting with Chef Henri and his staff and reassuring them they did a wonderful job, Louise had her morning meeting with the housekeeping manager. She also had to do a lot of reassuring in this meeting. Louise believed in supporting the people that you lead. She tried her best to know every employee's name and know things about them. She knew that a happy staff stayed happy when management cared and listened. Unfortunately, her grandmother didn't share this belief, so the past day with her staying at the estate had been a nightmare for the staff. She was a perfectionist, so was very critical of the staff's imperfections. Louise knew she would spend the next few days correcting any wrongs that her grandmother did.

The family would pack Grandmother off and send her back home to Florida in a few days. Louise had to make sure the entire staff didn't quit before then.

The morning flew by fast. Louise was standing at the front of the conference table at 10:30 a.m. wondering where her morning went. She wanted more time to rehearse the presentation again. And again. She didn't feel ready even though she had rehearsed the presentation at least thirty times in the past month. Her numbers were right, and she even hired a professional editor to look over it for grammar and spelling mistakes. She was ready, more than ready.

At least that's what she kept saying to herself. She tried to lessen the pressure by breathing deeply. She had to remember that the board moved slowly; they all wanted to defer to Grandmother. Louise looked up as Grandmother and Jamal walked into the room. She smiled and tried to send Jamal an "I'm sorry" look. She could tell by the weariness in his eyes that he had been with Grandmother all morning.

Grandmother was a regal woman. You wouldn't have expected her to have grown up 'barefoot and poor', as she always said, from rural Alabama. She stood at Jamal's shoulders but looked as though she was taller than him. Looking at Grandmother,

Louise knew she would age well. She had hair full of white in a top chignon and a red tailored suit with stockings and 1-inch heels. The white lace shawl around her and the wrinkles around her eyes were the only indicators of her age. Everything else screamed CEO, and Louise had to fight the growing dread that settled in her stomach.

"Good morning, Grandmother. How did you sleep last night?" she asked.

"Good morning, Louise. I slept well, thank you. I expected to see you at breakfast this morning."

"Sorry, grandmother, I had my usual duties to take care of. I usually grab something quick at home, anyway." Louise replied.

"All the money we spend on that French chef and you 'grab something quick' at home?" Grandmother tsked. "Well, I requested a pleasant lunch for us after the meeting today."

Louise continued to smile but cringed internally. She already had lunch prepared for after the meeting. Grandmother went behind her back and changed things all the time. She wanted to say that she already had a lunch planned for the past two months and had specialty items flown in so that her French trained chef could show off his skills. She wanted to yell that Grandmother should respect her leadership. She didn't, though. In a few minutes, she had to present a radical idea to the board and couldn't afford to lose it now.

"Thank you, grandmother. That was very kind of you." Gratefully, her parents walked in right at that moment.

"Mom, Dad, good morning!" she said, maybe a little too excitedly. Dad hugged grandmother and more family entered the room. It was getting time to start. Louise took a deep breath and look towards grandmother to start the meeting.

Promptly at 10 a.m., Grandmother called the meeting to order. As usual, the meeting started off with the previous minutes and old business. Louise only had to present the revenue from the new spa. The spa was doing well, with Louise having booked many girl's trips in the spring and summer. The fall and the winter were slower, but the warm months more than made up for it. Louise noted that during the spring/summer season, the hotel books full of those wanting to come for a spa weekend. She also mentioned that the bookings for next year were already filling up.

Louise hoped this tidbit would help in the next part of her presentation. Next, they talked about finances, which always dragged on. Around 12:30 p.m., Grandmother finally called for new business. Louise stood up and requested the floor.

She took a deep breath and looked at Jamal, who started passing out the packets. He gave her a reassuring smile, and she dove into her presentation. For the next twenty minutes, Louise was on top of her game. She gave the reports, pricing, and showed how this investment would not only grow the estate but would leave a legacy for the next two or three generations. Most of the board seemed into the presentation. A few questions came, but she answered them. She couldn't get a read from Grandmother, but she could never read her face.

She opened the floor for discussion and received accolades from her dad for the presentation, which she expected. What she didn't expect was Uncle Frank and his wife, Sarah. They both loved the idea of expansion and Uncle James shared he had been wanting to do something similar before he retired as general manager. Hearing this from Uncle James, whom she took the position of general manager from, was very encouraging.

"Thank you all." She said. "Should we call a vote, then?" She looked over to grandmother who face was still unreadable.

"I need to think some more about this, Louise." Grandmother interjected. "We need more conversation about what this expansion could mean. You want to take an additional mortgage out on the land? If I'm reading this right, the building of the structures could take two years and that is with favorable conditions. What if it takes longer, say, three or four years, for the additional spaces to be operational? That will change your revenue timeline. And change the payoffs for both the mortgages. We will pay the current mortgage off in a few years. Walter, you know the numbers. How long?"

"Yes, Mother, that is four years and ten months." Louise's father said.

"And you want to add another loan on top of this one?" Grandmother shot back at Louise. Louise nodded. "I don't know, Louise. This is a lot to take on currently. I would like to think more about the numbers. We can wait to vote on this at our spring meeting."

"But…" Louise tried to interject but didn't know what to say.

"Any other new business?" Grandmother dismissed Louise, even if Louise knew how to respond. Louise looked at her mom. She had a fierce look on her face that reminded Louise to be tough. Louise fixed her face into a placid smile and returned to her seat. As she did, her cousin Malcolm stood.

"I have new business," said Malcolm. "A great time for it, it seems."

He looked over at Louise. Louise guessed he must be mad she didn't run the expansion idea by him. Louise and Malcolm had a very complicated relationship. Malcolm was the first-born grandchild, a boy, and very spoiled. Louise was the second born and her parents only had her. Grandmother with her "traditional" view believed that only a Cummings should run the board and manage the estate. Her thinking was that eventually Louise would marry and change her name.

Grandmother didn't know that Louise would rather stay single forever than give up her title as general manager. Grandmother would have preferred Malcolm to take the reins after Uncle Frank retired. Malcolm wanted nothing to do with the day to day running of the estate. He only wanted to look as though he was in charge. There was the contention in their relationship. Malcolm acted as if he ran the estate, but Louise ran it. So, Malcolm expected Louise to run all her ideas by him first.

Malcolm continued with his thought. "I have been working with a consulting company for one of my clients. And I would like the company to come and do some consulting for us."

"What kind of consulting, Malcolm?" Uncle James, Malcolm's father asked.

"General consulting, to assist us with growth. Since Louise presented her idea of expanding, the firm could consult on if this would be a profitable idea for us. And give you some reassurance, grandmother." He smiled at grandmother.

"Malcolm, that sounds like an excellent idea. Don't you agree, Louise?" Grandmother said, not breaking her sight with Malcolm.

"If that would help you feel more comfortable with the expansion, then I guess so." Louise responded. Meanwhile, she glared at Malcolm for upstaging her. She was the GM, so he should have run this idea by her before presenting it to the board.

"Should we call a vote?" Malcolm asked.

"But what about the discussion? Can we get more information on the firm?" Louise said.

"All in favor of hiring a consulting company to assist with the expansion, please raise your hand." Grandmother said, cutting off Louise's questions. Hands raised, including Jamal's and her father's. She looked at dad and he mouthed 'sorry'.

"Those not in favor of hiring this company, please raise your hand." Grandmother said. Louise, her mother, and Uncle Frank raised their hands.

"Motion passed." Grandmother smiled; the first sign of emotion Louise saw all day. Luckily for Louise, there wasn't any other new business or much left for the meeting. She was too shocked and upset about what happened to pay much attention. After the meeting adjourned, she quickly went back to her office and locked the door.

CHAPTER 2

LOUISE WENT TO her lower left drawer for her emergency candy. She grabbed her favorite—peanut butter cups. Today she will need four. As she settled back in her chair to enjoy her snack, there came a knock at the door. *I don't want to deal with anyone right now.* If it was work related, they could send an instant message. The person knocked again as she finished her first cup.

"Sweetie, it's me, daddy." That back-stabber was the last person she wanted to talk to right now. She didn't answer back as he tried the door handle.

"Come on, pumpkin pie. Please open." Louise's dad gets sappier until she opens the door. She unlocked the door and let him in, locking it back. A full family run down was not something she was in the mood for. Returning to her desk, she took another bite of her second peanut butter cup.

"Don't let your mom see you eating that," her dad said. Her mom, Mary Cummings, was the slim athletic type who still ran marathons in her mid-sixties. It took years for her mom to accept that all body types were good and a size six could be as healthy as a size sixteen. Even though Louise and her mother had an understanding that she would let her happy, healthy, and well-adjusted daughter be, she still gave her dirty looks whenever she over-indulged.

"Well, mom isn't here," she said, biting into another cup.

"Don't be mad at me, sweetheart."

"Dad, why did you vote for that consulting firm? You always take her side."

"I wasn't taking anyone's side. It wouldn't hurt to have an outside entity look at the numbers to make sure we do the expansion right. You know your grandmother needs time for any decision she makes."

"But we don't need a consult. We have looked at the numbers a million times."

"And it might help to get an outside voice."

"Or another voice other than mine." She murmured.

"Louise, you know James and I trust your leadership. Neither one of us had any qualms about giving you the reins when he retired, and I focused more on the charity arm of Cummings Estate—"

"The charity! I should have brought up how we can use the cabins for the summer camp."

"Sweetie, there really wasn't anything else you could have said to sway your grandmother. You know she needs time to think."

"Not when it comes to Malcolm. She didn't even open a discussion for this consulting firm. We don't even know the firm's name."

"I'm sorry Louise. But it's not a bad idea. Would you have rejected it if it came from anyone other than Malcolm?" Louise forcibly stopped herself from rolling her eyes. Peacemaker dad to the rescue. The trouble of being a child of the middle child is that they always try to make peace when conflict happens.

"I guess, Daddy. But I still don't like him springing this on us without a discussion."

"Just like you sprang the expansion on him? You should have discussed it with Malcolm."

"Dad, Malcolm lives in L.A., he is a lawyer. He has exercised himself from the family business years ago. He isn't even the family lawyer anymore. So why do I have to run my ideas to him?"

"Because it's family."

"Dad, you don't understand."

"What don't I understand? Not being the favorite? Having a smart and capable older brother like James that took over the hotel effortlessly. Or having a fun-loving younger brother like Frank that everything came easy to."

Louise walked over to her dad and hugged him. She knew it was a lot of history and healing done in his generation. Her grandparents were amazing people, but they had flaws like all parents. Her dad spent a good chunk of his life trying to fit up to their high expectations. She knew he did everything out of love for the family.

"I'm still mad at you for voting for that consultant, but I forgive you." He laughed, recognizing the levity in her comment. He kissed her on her forehead and said, "give this company a chance, sweetheart. Please."

"Ok, daddy, I will try." She stepped back. "If you trust this, I will try. But if anything goes wrong—"

"You will boot them out of here, I know."

"I was a little out of it, so did anyone get any details from Malcolm?" Louise asked as she went back to sit at her desk.

"No, and we should have discussed the details. The holidays are coming up fast. I'm going to head to lunch. Are you coming?" she shook her head, opening another pack of the cups. "Ok then, I will try to get some more details from Malcolm. Don't be mad at your grandmother for too long. Love you, sweetie. And don't worry about locking it back. I'll keep the family away for a while."

"Thanks daddy."

IT WAS A week later before Malcolm gave them any details about the consulting firm that would be coming. Willis and Spencer consulting firm seemed like an excellent company from what Louise and Jamal could find online. Louise even reached out to the firm to get more information. The contact information from Malcolm gave the name of Carlos Hernández as the consultant. Louise couldn't reach Mr. Hernández herself, so she spoke with an assistant. Luckily for her, the assistant was very chatty and gave her information on Mr. Hernández. She left the conversation knowing that he was 'very attractive', very charming, and very good at his job. None of it mattered. Louise hoped to use this information to get more out of this consultant than he got out of her estate.

After a lot of back and forth with Malcolm, and then Malcolm's back and forth with the consulting company, they finally decided for the consultant to come at the beginning of December. Louise tried to put off the visit until after the new year, when it would be calmer at the hotel. The holiday season was busy, and the estate was almost full. Louise didn't want to worry about having a room reserved for an unwanted guest. She tried to save a few rooms for the family or special guests. She assigned one of them to Mr. Hernández, but didn't know how long he planned on staying, as Malcolm wouldn't confirm Mr. Hernández's leave date.

Louise got busy with the planning of the holidays, which included decorating the estate and the tree lightening ceremony.

The biggest feat was turning the beautiful mountain escape into a holiday wonderland. Every year they held a contest in town for someone to pick the theme. This year a young girl won with an ice princess theme. The decorators and staff enjoyed turning the hotel into the girl's movie fantasy.

Then December hit. And Mr. Hernández was due to come the following Monday. Louise got so busy with the holiday plans that she forgot to worry about the consultant. She walked down to the front desk to make sure the details of Mr. Hernández's arrival were perfect.

Her best friend, and recent employee, Harper, was on duty.

"Hey Harp, what are you doing here so early?" Louise rarely saw Harper while the sun was up. Harper worked the night shift. During the day, she was usually creating art.

"Hi Lou, I'm working for Patrick. Didn't they tell you? His wife went into labor this morning." She beamed.

"How exciting! No, I didn't know. I was in the back with over a hundred pounds of ice. They are sculpting an ice wave to look like it shot out of Alice's hands. That little girl is going to have the time of her life." Louise said.

"Cute. My mom and I finished her dress last week. Her parents were going to order it online, you know, from the character's store, but we knew it would be more special if it was homemade. And I was able to create little crystal snowflakes to add to it."

"I'm so excited. I know you aren't going to pull a double." Harper grinned. "Harper, that is over twelve hours."

"Girl, don't worry about it. I need to make some extra cash anyway. Making my dad something special this year."

"I don't want the labor police on me for overworking an employee. Even if the employee is my best friend."

"I will have a couple of breaks tonight. I promise no one will call the labor police."

Louise rolled her eyes and smiled. She and her best friend for all her life were as opposite as two people could get. Louise was short; Harper was tall. Louise was plus size, and Harper was thin. Louise was buttoned up and business like; Harper was a hippie with flowing, bluish-grey curly locks this week.

"I like the hair, by the way. Very on theme."

"Thanks. I have a reservation question." Louise came closer to the computer. "We have some last-minute reservations for the week before and after Christmas. I don't know who approved it, but we need three rooms for it."

"Mmm, let me see. We can put them in the rooms I have saved. I don't think any of my family is coming for Christmas. And if they do, then can stay with my folks. And it looks as though Mr. Williams wants to spend the holidays with us. He hasn't been here in years. He arrives on the 15th. I can put him in the last available room. Now we are all booked up." Louise looked up at Harper. "We should be good if no one else tries to make a reservation. I will have Jamal make sure the listings are closed."

"What about the last room? You usually have 5 rooms opened."

Louise sighed heavily before answering. "It's for the consultant the family hired. He will be with us for I'm not sure how long."

"Consultant? When did that happen?"

"At the board meeting. He is coming Monday, and I want to make sure his room is perfect. I also want to make sure his schedule is busy." She pulled up the itinerary. "I have him booked for a lot of activities in town. He can see how the town and the hotel work together. He will also be out of my hair."

"You are a sneaky little thing," Harper said while laughing.

"Clever is the word you mean."

CHAPTER 3

T HE NEXT MONDAY arrived, and the consultant was set to check-in that afternoon. Louise was in her black pantsuit and red top. She felt powerful in the suit. She was at the front desk with Harper, who was still covering for Patrick. They both had been standing there for an hour, waiting. Jamal had walked away. He also was nervous and kept walking to the front to catch sight of the visitor.

Around 2 p.m., Mr. Hernández finally arrived. Louise wasn't watching the door. She was looking at some purchasing receipts she needed to approve. She knew someone walked in because Harper grabbed her arm. When Harper pointed to the door, she protested. Louise's breath hitched a little, as the most handsome man she had ever seen was at the entrance.

The sun was at his back, causing him to glow a little. He was tall, and through his winter coat, you could see his muscular physique. His copper skin glowed as he looked up at the ceiling, noticing the artwork that was carved up there. His dark curly hair waved like the ocean. He then turned to look at them, and Louise held her breath as Harper tightened her grasp. His beautiful hazel eyes seemed to peer inside her soul. He then smiled. It was a wide smile full of perfect teeth and confidence. She heard Harper give a low whistle, which thankfully broke the spell.

He walked over; the smile turning more confident as he saw the effect he had on the ladies. "Good afternoon, ladies. I'm Carlos Hernández. I'm looking for Louise Cummings."

He reached the front desk and Harper let go of Louise, only to grab Mr. Hernández's hand.

"Hello." Louise heard the bass in Harper's voice. She knew by that her friend was smitten and on the prowl.

"Hello, Louise?"

"No," Louise had to pull Harper back, "I am Louise Cummings. It is nice to meet you."

Mr. Hernández's hands were smooth as silk and warm despite the cold outside. Louise told herself to get it together, remembering the assistant said this man was a charmer. She is not easily charmed.

"Harper, will you get Mr. Hernández checked in?" Harper finally shook herself and started typing on the computer.

"Of course, Louise." They all stood there, Louise trying to avoid Mr. Hernández's eyes and look busy. Harper was taking forever while trying to capture Mr. Hernández's attention. While he stared at Louise.

"I got you all checked in." Harper finally said.

Mr. Hernández turned his attention to her and grabbed his keycards. "Thank you, Harper, is it?"

"Yes." Harper answered and winked. "The elevators are down the hall to your right."

Louise was annoyed, but she also knew her best friend. There was no getting in between Harper and a new conquest. Louise gestured to the bellman on duty.

"Beau, Mr. Hernández is in room 526. Can you grab the rest of his bags, please?" Louise said.

"Carlos." Mr. Hernández said.

"Excuse me?"

"Mr. Hernández is my father. You can call me Carlos."

"Ok...um, Beau will handle what you need..." As he turned to walk towards the elevators, she called, "Mr. Hernández." She turned and headed to her office.

About ten minutes later, Jamal walked into Louise's office and sat down. He was all smiles, looking like the Cheshire cat.

"So, I hear Mr. Consultant is fine as heck! When can I meet him?"

"As far as I'm concern you can meet and keep him."

"Mmmm,...well! Mr. Fine didn't turn your head?"

"No!" Harper said from the doorway. "Don't worry, I'm on break. But Jay, she didn't even look at him. I mean *look*."

"Well, I can't wait to *look*." Said Jamal laughing.

"He was so dreamy. I'm going to give him a tour of the town." Harper said.

"Perfect," Louise said. "Anything to keep him out of my hair."

"Me thinks she protests too much," said Jamal.

"Right!" Harper said, laughing.

Louise rolled her eyes. "His attractiveness," both Harper's and Jamal's brows raised, "or not, doesn't matter. The fact remains that he is here to evaluate our hotel. He is going to make and give a report to people we don't know. And this report could affect our business negatively."

"That is rough," harper said, "but he still is fine." She and Jamal started laughing again. Louise couldn't help herself and she started laughing, too.

"Ok, I'll admit it. He is very, very...very attractive."

"Oooohhh" from the peanut gallery.

TUESDAY MORNING, LOUISE woke up to her normal schedule. Awake at 5:30 a.m., she took twenty minutes to pray and meditate, then did a ten-minute yoga routine. She ate a light breakfast, showered, and got dressed for the day. By 6:30 a.m., she was in her mirror checking herself and making sure everything was in place. She was ready for her four-minute walk up to the hotel where she always stopped to marvel at the ceiling artwork. As she took in a breath, readying herself for the day, a voice said, "Beautiful, isn't it?"

She turned to see Mr. Hernández sitting in a chair in the lobby. Louise was confused, as his itinerary didn't start until nine that morning.

"Good morning, Mr. Hernández." She said.

"Please call me Carlos." He stood.

She cleared her throat. "Mr. Hernández, how can I help you today?"

He smiled, and she did all she could not to melt into that smile. "Ms. Cummings, I noticed my itinerary was full of some amazing activities. One thing was missing."

"Oh, we missed something, I apologize. What is it?" Mr. Hernández was holding out the itinerary she had laminated, so she got closer to him and looked over it. He smelled amazing. She was losing the focus battle with this proximity.

"You. You are missing from the itinerary." She looked up at him, confused. "Ms. Cummings, I see that there are a lot of activities and tours of the estate and the town. But I came here as a consultant. So, I need time with the staff. I was told you got here at 6:30 a.m., so I started with you."

She stepped back. Mr. Hernández didn't fall for her busy schedule scheme to get him off her back. Her full focus on the position this man filled came back in full force. She steadied herself.

"Well, Mr. Hernández, I know you are consulting for Malcolm, so I created an itinerary that would show you the best of the Cummins Estate and the town that we support and supports us. If you have an issue with it, then I can have Jamal adjust it."

She walked towards her office. Mr. Hernández was on her heels. She turned to stare at him.

"Yes, Mr. Hernández, was there anything else?"

"I really wish you would call me Carlos." She didn't break her stare. She knew he was waiting for her to reciprocate. "Ms. Cummings then. I'll spend the morning with you. I'm already up and Jamal isn't here to adjust the itinerary."

"We have a lovely breakfast in the dining room."

"Ms. Cummings, you won't be able to avoid me on my entire trip. Let's get the business out of the way now, then the fun can come later." He flashed that smile again. She hoped that eventually it wouldn't influence her. That eventually wasn't this moment. She turned back to the direction of her office. He didn't follow this time.

"Well, come on if you are coming."

CHAPTER 4

AN HOUR AND a half later, when Jamal finally made it to work, Mr. Hernández had turned her office into his second home. He had completely taken over half of her desk with a laptop and assorted papers, ordered a small breakfast with lots of coffee, and was currently reading through her expansion presentation when Jamal came to her door.

"Morning boss. What's going on here?" She and Mr. Hernández looked up at him and she saw his face brighten at the sight of him. She tried to gesture to him to keep a straight face, but Jamal was all smiles.

"Good morning," he said as he walked up, holding out his hand. "You must be the famous Mr. Hernández."

"Carlos, please." Mr. Hernández stood and shook Jamal's hand. "And you must be Malcolm's brother, also the assistant GM of this lovely estate."

"Why yes, I am. And *you* can call me Jamal." Louise signaled a finger across her throat to Jamal.

"Jamal, did you need something from me? Alone?" Louise asked.

"Oh no, boss, looks like you have your hands full. I will leave you two alone." Jamal walked out and towards his office. Louise jumped up and followed him. She closed the door behind them.

"Save me, please."

"What?" Jamal laughed, sitting at his desk.

"Did you see my desk? He moved in. I need you to save me and take him away. Anywhere."

"While I do like the thought of someone offering a man for me to take, I don't have any plans with him until tomorrow."

"He is supposed to see the setup for the winter festival this morning. Saw right through my schedule, and now he wants more time with me, us, the staff. He has only been in my office for a little while, and did you see what he did?"

"He is a messy one. And way cuter than what Harper said. Anyway, I have a busy morning. I don't have time today. "

"Don't worry about it. I will take over your schedule."

"With your already busy schedule, you'll want to sit in the community meetings I have today and the finance planning meeting with the charity. Or do you want me to take Carlos?"

"Oh, gosh no! He doesn't need to 'consult' on those. You are right. I will pawn him off to the different departments."

"True, he is here to consult. No matter how much we hate it. So let him consult."

"Well, can he 'consult' from your office?"

Jamal laughed loudly. "He seems very much at home in your office. I wouldn't want to disturb him."

"Jamal, this isn't funny! He is a mess. My office smells like eggs and coffee."

Jamal stood and walked towards Louise. He put his hands on her shoulders and turned her around.

"I know this is hard for little Miss Perfect," he said as he opened his door, "but he is your mess to clean up now."

He pushed her out the door and turned her to her office.

"They have kicked me out of better places than this." She said.

"You haven't, and that is the problem. Relax, Lou. Have fun with that cutie!" he yelled the last part.

"Shhhhhhh! Jamal, this is not funny."

He continued to laugh as he went back into his office. She stormed into her office, seething. This anger was what she needed. This Mr. Hernández wouldn't charm her. And that bit of frustration from Jamal helped.

Mr. Hernández looked up when she sat at her desk. He had a glint in his eye like he heard Jamal. She ignored him and looked through her email. He cleared his throat, and she looked back at him.

"This presentation is great. Very detailed. They did not approve this?"

His genuineness shocked her. The first bit of genuine she sensed from him.

"No, it wasn't. My Grandmother wanted more time to think about the plans and look over the numbers. It's a big expansion."

"Is that why I'm here, then?"

"No, Malcolm planned for your company to come, anyway. His idea coming after I presented the expansion was my dumb luck, I guess." She rolled her eyes.

"Or it was my good luck." He smiled that smile. Louise's stomach took a nose-dive again. She was so happy that she had better control of her face. "It is a big expansion, but looking at these figures, it would benefit the hotel immensely."

"Thank you. That is what I think. It takes the board a little longer to agree on big decisions like this."

"Well, I love this expansion idea and will add this to the report. My company will love your plans."

"Thank you again." Louise returned to her email to control the heat that was rising to her face. His compliments got to her. She was used to her family and staff complimenting her, but it was reassuring hearing a stranger complement her ideas for the hotel.

Another hour passed with them both working in a comfortable silence. Mr. Hernández's mess still annoyed Louise. Occasionally, she would straighten up his papers and place them on his laptop. He would apologize, put them up, then twenty minutes later, a new stack slowly spread closer to her side of the desk.

"If you hurry, you can make it to the setup for the festival." She finally said.

"Like I said before, Ms. Cummings, while you gave me a busy schedule full of amazing things to do around the hotel, none of these things would allow me to learn about the estate or the business. So, I will hang with you today."

Louise took a deep, angry breath. Mr. Charming wasn't so charming, she realized.

"Fine, Mr. Hernández. I am going to meet with the housekeeping supervisor now. I usually meet with the various departments on a weekly basis."

"That is great." He stood. "Let's go."

After meeting with the housekeeping supervisor, Louise and Mr. Hernández went back to her office for a working lunch. They continued to work, and she ordered some sandwiches. While Mr. Hernández was looking through the major projects, she was doing her regular duties. The spa addition was the first thing she had him look at.

Louise was glad that he was quiet while they worked that afternoon. It still annoyed her that he could charm Mrs. Thomas, the supervisor of housekeeping. Mrs. Thomas had been with the resort for thirty-plus years and was tough, but fair. Louise liked her but Mrs. Thomas gave her a hard time because she knew her from birth. She was mad that Mr. Hernández came in and had Mrs. Thomas blushing like a young girl five minutes into the conversation. Louise had to find some way to get this man off her back.

After a couple of afternoon meetings with the decorators and the party planner, Louise was ready to call it a day. Mr. Hernández was on her heels the whole time. She was especially glad to leave the estate and Mr. Hernández for the day. She gathered his papers and placed them on his laptop.

"Thank you, but you don't have to do that." He said.

"It's almost five. Time to wrap up the day."

"I'm good. The west coast is still in the middle of their day. I'll work here. You can go home."

"Mr. Hernández, this is still my office. You can work from your room." She continued to straighten up the mess that he made in her office. His suit jacket was thrown over her couch, along with some snacks he ordered.

"You don't have to clean anything. Can't you have house-keeping do that?"

"I can, Mr. Hernández, but I don't. I like to keep my space clean and not put more work on others," she said, while handing him his jacket.

"I'm sorry," he smiled. "I am a bit of a mess." He stood up and started helping her gather the mess. He even grabbed the trash out of the bin.

"I didn't mean for you..."

"Hey, my mother would have a fit if she saw the hurricane I created. What she doesn't know is that I have a housekeeper that worries about my messiness. I invaded your space, so I should have been more respectful."

"You are fine."

"I *am* fine," he winked at her.

"I didn't mean that. I meant you are good...I mean, no worries about the mess."

He chuckled. "You don't have to excuse it, but tomorrow I will do better. Don't think I didn't notice you eyeing me all day and putting my stuff away."

Louise turned away, a little embarrassed. She was usually more direct but didn't know how to react to this new stranger upsetting her life.

"Thank you for that. Anyway, have a good night. By the way, look at your itinerary. There are some fun things in town this evening."

"Will you be there?"

"Maybe."

He gathered up the last of his things and held out his hand. Louise grasped it and they held on to each other a little too long.

"Well, I hope to see you tonight." He said as he let her hand go. He smiled that winning smile, then left her office. Louise stood there, her arm still a little extended. Her mind turned to mush, and she couldn't do anything. Jamal waking in a few minutes to her still in that state.

"Are you ok Louise?" He stepped in front of her and snapped. "Louise!"

"Hum, oh Jamal, where did you come from?"

"I've been here for a few seconds while you were in space. Where exactly did you go? Planet Carlos?"

"Shut up! No such thing. I was thinking about all I need to do tomorrow."

"Yeah, ok, I'll accept that lie."

She walked behind her desk and start gathering her stuff.

"Are you coming to the tree lighting ceremony tonight?" he asked.

"Maybe."

"Maybe? I only asked out of tradition. You never come to the town's ceremony. You always claim to be too busy."

"I usually am too busy. This year I have a little time and I may come."

He looked at her with an eyebrow raised. She really hadn't planned on going to the town's ceremony. She had plenty of things that she could and should do this evening. It would be nice for her to spend some time with her parents and friends in town. At least that is how she reasoned with herself.

CHAPTER 5

THAT EVENING, LOUISE dressed in one of her many Christmas outfits. She loved the holiday season and the estate always reflected that. So did her clothes after work. She had on Christmas green pants and green and gold "ugly" sweater and a green elf hat. She completed the outfit with her green tree decorated coat and ornament earrings. In town, she found her parents on a bench drinking hot cocoa.

"Hey Mom and Dad." She kissed each on the cheek.

"Well, if it isn't my long-lost daughter. I thought you moved to Bora Bora or somewhere." Her mom said.

"Mom, don't be so dramatic."

"Well, I haven't seen you since Thanksgiving. You are not still mad about the meeting, are you? Walt, you said you both talked."

"Mom, calm down. We talked. I'm not mad anymore. I have been busy."

"Louise, you live twenty minutes down the road. You haven't been that busy."

She sat next to her mom and give her a big hug. "I have been that busy."

"Speaking of busy," her father started, "how was the first day with the consultant?" Louise looked over at her father and mouthed a thank you.

"It went. He stayed by my side the whole day. I'm behind on some things."

"I don't like this. It's unnecessary." Her mother said.

"Mary...," said her father.

"Walter...it's the truth. Everyone trusts how Louise is running the estate. At least everyone should." Her mother crossed her arms. Louise gave her another big hug. She can forget how wonderful it feels to have someone defend you.

"Thanks mom. I was upset at first. I'm still upset a little. But if this makes grandmother feel comfortable, then...anyway it's done. He is here."

"Where here exactly?" asked her mother.

"He is staying at the estate. He can get a front row view on how we run the place."

"Other than hating that he is here, how is it?" her father asked.

"It wasn't too bad. He didn't fall for the "busy work" itinerary Jamal and I created. He did like my presentation for the expansion. Said he would put it in his report."

"Of course, he liked your presentation, baby. It was amazing."

"Thanks mom."

Music started from the bandstand, letting the crowd know that the ceremony would be starting.

"Your mom and I will enjoy everything from this bench. Why don't you get a little closer? Over there with the young kids."

"Daddy, I haven't been a 'young kid' in a while now." she laughed.

"Well, get on anyway so your daddy can talk sweet nothings in my ear." Mom said

"Ew!" Louise jumped up and headed towards the crowd. She loved that her parents were still all over each other. She didn't want to see it.

In the middle of town, there was a park that they call the town square. It was a small park, but the tree stood at the edge with a stage big enough for about five or six people and a small band. She found Jamal and his husband, Silas, standing near the tree. They both gave her a hug. Silas was as tall as Jamal but with olive skin. His features were sharp, but he was the warmest person who anyone could ever meet.

"So, you made it." Jamal said.

"Yes, I wanted to see my parents."

"Mmm hum." He said.

"Jay, leave her alone. This girl needs to get off that estate. Don't make fun of her for doing it or we won't see her until the groundhog says so."

They all laughed. The band started playing a Christmas carol and the crowd all joined in. Twenty minutes later, they were watching a band from the high school play a rock version of another Christmas carol when Louise felt a tap on her shoulder. She turned to see Mr. Hernández standing behind her. Her stomach and heart both jumped. In her relaxed state, she forgot to control the smile on her face. He smiled back at her with his winning smile. Her stomach leaped again as she tried to regain control of her face.

"Hello, Carlos." Jamal said. "How are you doing this fine evening?"

"Hey Jamal, I'm doing well, thank you. How are you? And you Ms. Cummings?" he said.

"I am doing well," said Jamal. "I would like you to meet my husband, Silas. Si, this is the consultant we all have been talking about."

"Hello, nice to meet you." Silas said as he shook Mr. Hernández's hand. Louise still hadn't found her voice, so she stood there with a stupid smile on her face. She tried to wake up her senses. Mr. Hernández looked extra handsome tonight. He had on jeans and a pea coat that showed off his frame. A frame that Louise had spent the whole day trying to ignore. His eyes seemed to glitter in the lights that were hanging around them.

"Great!" Louise yelled as she realized she interrupted Jamal mid-sentence.

"You ok Lou?" Jamal asked.

"Yes, I was saying I was great. Thank you, Mr. Hernández." She said. Jamal and Silas exchanged looks. Louise wanted to correct the assumption that she liked Mr. Hernández, but he was standing right there, his attention focused on her.

"I'm glad to see you. The town is beautiful." Mr. Hernández directed towards her. She could see Silas pulling Jamal away out of the corner of her eye. She wanted to tell them to stay, but it was taking all her composure to keep the silly grin off her face.

"I can't take credit for the town but thank you. They do a wonderful job during the holidays."

"They have done a great job. It gives all the small-town feels you want. Very Bedford Falls."

"Bedford Falls?"

"Yes, from—"

"It's a Wonderful Life," they said in unison.

"It's my favorite movie!" she said.

"It's also one of my favorites. My mom and dad would have us watch it every Christmas eve. They wanted us to remember to keep family close and to stay humble. And to believe in angels." They smiled at each other. She noticed his eyes seemed to soften when he talked about his parents. They turn to the stage as the mayor got to the podium to give a speech.

Louise noticed that Mr. Hernández was standing super close to her. She tried to step away but bumped into the person next to her, stumbling. Mr. Hernández grabbed her arm to steady her, and she looked up into his eyes, mind turning to mush again. He smiled, but it was softer than his 'winning' smile. She imagined herself falling into that smile.

"Ten, nine, eight, seven…" the yells of the surrounding people broke the spell she was momentarily under. She shook off her imaginings and remembered why this man was in her life now. She had to hate him. As he let her arm go, she stiffened against him.

"Three, two, ONE!" the mayor hit the switch and the tree lights glowed. They were bright and beautiful. The town's tree decorators worked with the ones at the estate so the town would match the theme chosen for the estate. The lights were white and light blue with little snowflake crystals that glimmered, and the tree topper was a large angel with snowflake wings.

Louise smiled to herself. The tree was as beautiful as she imagined it would be. It would match perfectly with the theme at the estate. She was happy that she came out to the ceremony. She hadn't been to it in years. Priorities at the estate consumed most of her time. She felt Mr. Hernández's eyes on her. She turned to him when the mayor called her name.

"Louise Cummings, everyone!" Mayor Shields said. Louise didn't know what she said before that, so she waved in a circle at everyone.

"No Louise, come up here. Thank you for all the hard work you and the staff at the estate do for us."

Louise felt butterflies, happy that Mr. Hernández wasn't the culprit. She didn't enjoy being the center of attention. It was easier playing in the background to let others shine for their good work. She approached the podium even though she wanted to run to her car.

"Thank you so much, Louise, for everything you and your family do for our town." Mayor Sheila Shields said into the mic.

"I'm going to kill you, Shelia." Louise whispered. Shelia Shields, like most of the town, knew Louise her whole life. Sheila graduated a couple of years before Louise and briefly dated at least two of her cousins.

"Thank you everyone. But the accolades should go to you all for making the town look amazing. I also want to thank Alice," she waved to Alice who she found in the crowd, "for our theme this year. Alice, your idea is wonderful, and I can't wait to show you and the town how the estate will look. Thank you all!" she waved to the crowd and made her way off the stage.

She pointed herself away from the tree, and Mr. Hernández, and hurried towards her car. Her parents were standing at the edge of the crowd and stopped her.

"I'm so happy for you." Her mother exclaimed and bear hugged her.

"For what, mom?"

"For being my special little girl." Louise groaned but held on to her mother.

"Impressive speech, Cuz!" Jamal and Silas joined the group. Louise was getting nervous. She wanted to get back home before Mr. Hernández caught up with them.

"Thanks Jamal, but you should have gone up there instead. Every knows you are the ham of this family."

"Why, I'm shocked!" Jamal touched his chest. Everyone else laughed at him. Louise hugged her mom and dad again and blew kisses as she walked away.

She made it to the sidewalk before she heard her name called, turning to see Mr. Hernández jogging towards her. She sighed and put on a placid smile.

"Hi, again. You are the only one that lives on the estate. If you don't mind, I need a ride back." He said.

"How did you get here?"

"I caught a ride with Beau. He was off duty and was coming to town. I was about to look at one of my rideshare apps when I saw you walking to your car. And I'm not sure if I would get a ride this late."

She rolled her eyes. "We are a small town, but we don't completely shut down at night."

Just then, the stringed lights around the park turned out, disproving her point. Mr. Hernández smirked.

"Sure, you can ride with me."

"Thanks. I have a couple of questions, anyway." They began walking towards her car.

"Mr. Hernández, no offense, but can they wait until tomorrow? I'm off now and don't want to talk about work."

"No problem. Since we are off duty, call me Carlos, Louise."

She looked up into his grin. She couldn't help but to smile but she turned away, hoping he wouldn't see it.

"Alright, Carlos, my car is up here."

She began walking down the sidewalk. Carlos turned and walked back to the park. He headed towards the cocoa cart.

"Where are you going?"

"I was told that the best hot chocolate I will ever have is here. I must try it before we leave."

"Hot Cocoa," she begrudgingly started following him

"Excuse me."

"We call it hot cocoa. It's better than regular 'hot chocolate'."

"Then I definitely need to try it."

They made it to the cart and stood in line behind a few people. The tree was still lit even though the stringed lights were off.

They were still quite a few people milling around. She noticed that two stores were still open. She smiled to herself.

"What's that smile for?" Carlos asked.

Louise motioned to the antique store behind the cart. She pointed to another store to the right of the square, laying her hand on his forearm.

"See, not so small of a town." He burst out in a laugh. She smiled, enjoying the hearty and loud timbre of his voice. He had done nothing but that "winning" smile of his all day. It was refreshing to see behind the front. She looked down at her hand still on his arm and quickly pulled it back, looking away. She tried to erase the feel of his muscular arm under her fingers.

"You are right, not such a small town after all."

They got to the window, and he ordered two large hot cocoas. When they were ready, he gathered both and pointed to a nearby empty bench. They sat enjoying the silence of the night, sipping their drinks.

"Well?" she finally asked.

"Mmmm. It is the best hot cocoa I have ever had." He smiled. She smiled back at him. "So, you like Christmas much?" he gestured to her outfit.

"Yes, doesn't everybody?" she laughed.

"Many people do, but I don't think as much as you."

"This time of year is so much fun. I don't get to wear things like this at work, so I clock out from work and clock into—"

"Mrs. Claus." He interrupted, laughing.

"Yes, at night I clock into my role as Mrs. Claus. Well, my role as an elf. If you couldn't tell by my height."

"A secret elf in our midst. Can't wait to tell my nieces and nephew that I met an actual elf."

"I can sign an autograph for you." She laughed and looked into his eyes again. They were warm and glowing despite the dark.

He put his arm on the back of the bench. She almost snuggled into him when she remembered this wasn't a date. This was two coworkers, not even coworkers, business partners. She jumped up from the bench.

"We better get back." She forced a yarn. "Morning will be here before we know it."

She looked around her for a place to put her cup. He grabbed it from her and took both their empty cups to a nearby trash bin. He then offered her his arm. She walked past him and his offered arm and quickly made it to her car. He was attempting to walk to her side of the car, but she slipped in before he could open her door for her. She wouldn't deal with him being gorgeous and a gentleman.

The car ride was quiet. Carlos tried to start a couple of conversations, but she kept her answers clipped. She parked in her driveway and got out the car.

"Follow that path to the estate and you will be good. Good night." She was at her door and had it unlocked and closed behind her in three minutes flat. Taking a deep breath, she wanted to see if he walked on to the estate but didn't want to risk him knowing she was looking. She had to plan for the next day. Back to business, as usual. She would not see Carlos, Mr. Hernández, outside of work again. Her brain couldn't handle that.

CHAPTER 6

T HE NEXT MORNING, she wore her most impressive, tailored suit, the one that made her feel like the CEO of a large corporation. She put on her dark mahogany lipstick because it made her feel powerful. She looked in the mirror and nodded to herself. Louise Cummings didn't play any games. This Louise Cummings ran an entire estate; she had over one hundred employees that she managed. This Louise sat on the board of directors and had ideas. This Louise didn't worry about hazel eyes or beautiful smiles with amazingly white teeth. He probably had his teeth whitened, anyway. Had to as much coffee as he drank.

Louise headed to the estate. She stopped at the entrance and looked up at the ceiling, closing her eyes to feel even more resolve of why she did this. She stood there longer than she usually did. Someone clearing their throat was the only thing that broke the spell. Carlos. Mr. Hernández was sitting in the same chair as the day before.

"Good morning, Louise."

She rolled her eyes. "Mr. Hernández, you don't have to be here this early."

"So, we are back to that again?" She began walking to her office. "If you are here at 6:30, then I am here at 6:30." He said.

She made it to her office and sat behind her desk, turning on her computer and settling in. He started the settle in too but didn't take up as much space as the previous day.

"What's on our schedule for today, Ms. Cummings?" she was going to lose an eye for rolling them so much in his presence.

"I have a meeting with Chef Henri and his assistant kitchen manager. You can sit in on that. It's not until ten, though, so if you need to grab breakfast, go ahead."

"We can grab breakfast together."

"I ate at home. You can go ahead. I like to use the quiet time to read emails."

"Great, I need to read some emails and send a couple of reports. Do you mind if I get some coffee?"

She rolled her eyes again. They were getting a lot of exercise.

"I'll order you a pot." He smiled as she called for the coffee.

The day went smoothly again. After the meeting with the chef, Mr. Hernández stayed with the staff to look over their books. It kept him out of her hair for most of the afternoon. Mr. Hernández enamored chef Henri's assistant manager, of course. She was about the same age as Louise and usually professional, but she flirted with Mr. Hernández shamelessly. Louise choked down the feelings of jealousy that tried to come up. She wasn't jealous, as that would be dumb. She didn't want to be seen shamelessly flirting and giggling around Mr. Hernández.

As the day ended, Louise was very proud of herself. She stayed professional all day with Mr. Hernández. He was packing up to head back to his room.

"I was thinking of taking a tour around the town. It was beautiful the day before, and how many chances does one person get to tour Bedford Falls?"

"That is a good idea." She started heading to the door.

"I would need a tour guide."

"I don't think so. The town is straight forward."

"But I don't want to get lost."

"If you use a car service or rideshare, we only have two or three drivers. They will give you a great tour. That is usually what I suggest."

They were both at the door now and he was looking down at her. No smile, just intense eyes. She stepped out the door to break the stare. She stared looking down the hall for help. Thankfully, Jamal stepped out of his office at that moment.

"Jamal!" she said, a little too loud.

"Hey Lou, headed home? Oh, hi Carlos. Sorry I missed you today, but I have us rescheduled for tomorrow to meet."

"No problem, Jamal. I enjoyed my kitchen tour and seeing what the chefs were up to."

"Speaking of tours," Louise said, "Mr. Hernández wants to tour the town this evening. If you are free, that would be great for him to get a more personal tour other than a rideshare driver."

"I'm free. I need to check with Silas." Jamal and Louise looked at Mr. Hernández. He had a new look on his face that Louise wasn't sure what it meant. He quickly changed it to that winning smile.

"I don't want to put you out. I wanted to explore the town more."

"No problem, Carlos. Let me text Silas and tell him to expect a guest for dinner."

Jamal turned around to text Silas, and Louise smiled up at Mr. Hernández. His earlier look was back. It seemed a little like confusion and amusement.

"Since you are taken care of, I'll see you tomorrow. And you don't have to be there first thing. I think you will meet with

Jamal around 9 a.m., so get some rest. Sleep in a little." She started walking and gave him a tiny wave.

"Thank you, Louise," she froze and looked back at him. He was smiling with a determination in his eye. "I'll see you in the morning. First thing."

She stormed away. She thought she could hear him laughing at her back.

THE REST OF the week into the next went the same way. Mr. Hernández was sitting in his same chair every morning when she arrived. They would work quietly the first part of the morning, then he would follow her during her daily duties. Louise rarely took a day off, so she would be there on Saturdays and Sundays during her regular schedule. Mr. Hernández was even there to greet her during her weekend shift. The days seemed to go easier. They got along in a comfortable silence. Louise stayed extra professional, and Mr. Hernández did the same.

He only ever asked her off the estate one more time. Saturday evening, he asked her about the town's entertainment. She couldn't help him because she hadn't been out on a weekend night-any night since before she came back from college. Harper was getting off around eight and offered to show him around, wink, wink. Louise knew that Harper would have a new love affair by the end of the night, so she bid him a good night and headed home.

Louise had to admit to herself that she was a little jealous. Not of Harper, of course. She was used to Harper and her love affairs. A little jealous of being stuck in her self-imposed matronliness, she should have gone out. Not to be around Mr. Hernández, but to be around people her own age. She was so wrapped up in the estate's management that she never allowed herself to have fun, the result of being available twenty-four hours a day for her guests and her staff. She was fine. At least, that is what she continued to tell herself.

That Sunday, Harper texted her a skull emoji. That emoji let Louise know that Harper's love affair with Mr. Hernández was DOA. She couldn't help the big grin that came onto her face. One that Mr. Hernández inquired about.

"Good news?" he asked.

"No, I mean, um, just a friend and a private joke." She quickly texted Harper to ask what happened.

"Oh, with that smile it must be from a male 'friend'."

"No! I don't have a boyfriend or anything like that! It is from my best friend, Harper."

Harper texted back that he wasn't interested. Their other friend in the group message, Angie, sent a laughing emoji.

"Harper is nice. A little forward, but nice. I do owe you an apology." Mr. Hernández explained.

"Do you?"

"Your town has a great nightlife. But Harper mentioned you don't get out much to know."

She quickly texted back.

> **LOUISE:** You told him I don't go out?

"I don't. I'm usually resting. Also, I like to be available for any emergencies. If something happens it usually will on a Saturday night." Louise said to Mr. Hernández.

She turned back to her computer, pretending to look at something. Harper texted back to the group.

> **HARPER:** All he could do was ask about you.
> Love you, bestie, but that is a mood killer.

Louise had to bite her lip to not smile at that text. Angie texted the heart eyes kissy emoji. She finally put her phone in her desk drawer.

"Did the conversation get boring?" Carlos inquired.

Louise hoped she wasn't outwardly blushing. Thank goodness for dark skin. But her heart was trying to beat out of her chest. She didn't want to believe that Mr. Hernández was asking about her about anything other than work.

"No, they are distracting."

"They?"

"Both of my best friends. Harper, who you met, and Angie, she lives out of town."

"You have friends outside of Sacamore?"

"Yes," she smiled. "Angie grew up here. We both went out of state to college. She stayed in her college town."

"Why did you end up coming back home?"

"There wasn't a question of me staying. Texas was great. Warmer and more sunshine than here. The people were great too. They were super friendly and 'southern', so I felt at home. But everything I did, do, it's for Cummings Estate. I rushed to get back here."

"It is a beautiful estate. I can see why you would want to get back. But you had no other plans? What did you want to be when you were a kid?"

She giggled. "Other than a brief stint of really wanting to be an elf as a kid, there was nothing I wanted to do besides work at the estate. In the summers, instead of working at the local ice cream shop, I delivered room service orders. I was a bellhop, a maid, washed dishes, pretty much anything you could do I did it. This place is, and has always been, magic for me."

She smiled to herself.

"I love the passion you have for Cummings Estate." Mr. Hernández said. "That makes my job easier. I don't have to worry about you being apathetic during this process."

"No apathy for me when it comes to the estate. But you have been here a few days. I still don't understand what you do.

Mr. Hernández laughed. "I guess that first day we didn't get into the meat of why I'm here."

He looked pointedly at her. Louise guessed it was her fault that Mr. Hernández spent much of his time fighting with her to get a little information. She hitched her shoulders, and he continued.

"What I'm doing now is observing your day-to-day operations. I'm looking at how the estate runs. I will also need to look at your finances, mortgage details, gross yield, et cetera. When I'm done with my review, I will present to you and the board any recommendations that I have that may help improve the running of the estate. This can be a tense process. Many clients give me a lot of pushbacks. I assure you that my company and I have your business' best interest in mind. I know it's hard to trust a stranger, but I hope you will."

He ended on his 'winning' smile that made Louise not want to trust him. She guessed her face showed her mistrust because he said. "I'm here to help, Ms. Cummings."

CHAPTER 7

ON TUESDAY, AFTER another successful meeting with Mrs. Thomas, Louise and Mr. Hernández settled back into her office. Louise couldn't believe that she was getting more comfortable with him being with her all day. Since he was neater, she started not to mind his presence.

Around noon, she picked up the phone to order them lunch. Her usual lunch consisted of a turkey sandwich and a side of carrots or a side salad. She wanted to keep the lunch light because she didn't want to nap the afternoon away. The first day, Mr. Hernández wasn't excited about their meager portions, but he hadn't complained about the lunches. Today, he put his hand on the digits so she couldn't dial out.

"No." He was also shaking his head.

"What?"

He got up and took the receiver out of her hand and hung up the phone. He then took her hand and urged her to stand.

"I can't do another turkey sandwich. Come with me ... please." He pulled her out of the office and towards the dining room.

"What is happening?" Louise tried to control her shock, so her voice came out squeaker than usual. Mr. Hernández stopped and let go of her hand. Louise was a little disappointed by his letting go.

"I have a surprise for you. It has come to my attention that you only eat lunch in your office. A boring and sad little lunch." He continued walking. She followed along.

"You also always eat breakfast and dinner at home. I thought I would see you at least in the evenings for dinner, but no. You pay for an award-winning French-trained chef and rarely eat his cooking. Today we remedy that.

"Mr. Hernández, we can't. I'm way too busy for a non-working lunch." He stopped again, this time looking into her eyes. He gave his winning smile. It had been days since he used that smile on her. She forgot how memorizing an effect it was.

"Ms. Cummings, you have enough time to take thirty minutes to have a decent lunch. Now please, shall we?"

When he stopped, they were already at the entrance of the dining room. She nodded. He opened the door for her. She walked in and towards the closest empty table. The dining room wasn't that full, so they would have a table away from others. Mr. Hernández shook his head and held out his arm for her. This time, she held it. He led her to one of the private dining suites. In the room was a table elegantly set for two and a server standing to the side.

"I thought this was a simple lunch."

"If you are going to eat, why not eat in style?" He went to hold her chair out for her. She sat in it, suppressing her smile. He even dramatically put her napkin in her lap. She couldn't help but to laugh at that. He sat across from her and the server lit the candles.

"Are you sure this will only be a thirty-minute lunch?" she asked.

"Maybe forty-five minutes. And before you say anything, I

checked your calendar. You don't have a meeting until 2 p.m. Anything else that is pressing, I promise to stay as late as you need to tonight."

She relaxed back into her chair. She couldn't remember the last time she didn't have a meal in front of a screen. Even for her breakfasts and dinners, she checked her emails or the estate's social media accounts. If she had a lunch with Jamal or Harper, she still stayed glued to her phone. She remembered her phone and didn't feel it in her pockets. She left it on her desk.

"I forgot my phone." She said.

"Good. I don't have mine either."

"But what if..."

"Jamal knows we are having lunch. And here comes Chef Henri. He knows where you are. If anything happens, we will find you."

Louise took a deep breath, trying to suppress her rising irritation. Mr. Hernández was making a kind gesture, but she didn't like to be outside of her routine. Chef Henri greeted them and offered their first dish as she tried to relax.

"I wanted to keep it very simple for you today," Chef Henri said, his French accent still coming through even though he has been here for years, "a salad for the first course. I present a goat cheese and roasted beet salad."

"Thank you, Chef Henri." Louise said. Chef Henri bowed and walked out the door to the kitchen.

"I'm not a huge goat's cheese fan. I'm sure you all eat goat cheese all the time in California."

Mr. Hernández smiled his softer smile, the genuine one. Louise hated she was learning his features so well.

"We have a lot of goat cheese and milk. It's not my favorite either. But I will never tell Chef that. The other day, I saw his temper flare when someone sent a dish back."

"Someone had the nerve to send a dish back?" she laughed. "That wasn't my grandmother, of course."

"Your grandmother doesn't like his cooking?"

She shook her head. "She thinks it's too rich." Mr. Hernández joined in on the laughter. "It's really hard to please grandmother."

"For what it's worth, I think the food is excellent."

"I'm glad you have been enjoying it."

"Why don't you eat more at the estate?" he asked

"I don't know. I'm used to my routine, I guess. I want to be available, but I also enjoy having my personal space. And I experiment with recipes at night."

"You cook?"

"Why is that such a shock? Yes, I cook."

"You are so dedicated to your job. Most of the women I know don't cook. Not that it's a problem."

"Does your girlfriend cook?" She looked at her food and took a bite. She couldn't believe she asked him that.

"No girlfriend to cook for me. I usually eat out or get my mother's cooking."

She put another couple of forkfuls in her mouth in order not to smile at that revelation. When she finished chewing, she spoke again.

"You said you have nieces and nephews. Do you come from a big family?"

"Yes. It's only my brother and me, but we have a lot of uncles and aunts and tons of cousins. Most of them are back in the Dominican Republic, where my parents are from."

"Have you been in California your whole life?"

"No, I was born in New York. We moved to L.A. when I was about 6 or 7. So I am more of a Cali boy than I like to admit. You were born in Sacamore, right?"

"Born and raised."

"And you never left?"

"No, except for the years I went to college and got my master's. Then, I ran back home." The server came to clear their dishes.

"I wanted to ask you a question." Louise said when the server was done. Mr. Hernández raised his eyebrows. "What did you want to be when you were a kid? I don't imagine boys in California dream of being consultants."

He laughed. "No, I didn't want to be a consultant. Nor did I want to be an elf. I wanted to be the usual—a firefighter, police officer, professional surfer. My mom and dad owned a bodega back in Brooklyn, so I briefly tried to be an entrepreneur."

"I've always wanted to surf. But we don't get many waves here." They both laughed.

"There aren't a lot of chances to surf here. If you ever make it to L.A., I will take you." He winked, and she lost all her senses. She took a gulp of water to bring herself back to professional Louise.

"So, how did you end up as a consultant?" she said, steering the conversation back to a safe topic.

"Very simple story." he began. "I was looking for a job and applied. I started in the mailroom. While delivering mail, I saw people in suits, looking professional, and I didn't want to stay in the mailroom. With no degree, it was difficult to move up in the company. I went to night school to get my degree. My natural charisma and charm worked well for the consultant position."

She rolled her eyes at the last statement. He laughed again.

"I'm I not supposed to know that I'm charismatic and charming?"

"You don't have to brag about it."

"I have to brag about it. You seem immune to my charms. How else will you know?"

Louise knew that Mr. Hernández was joking. At least she thought he was joking. Why would he want her to be charmed by him? She shook the thoughts off. Of course, he would want her charmed. He wanted to charm everyone and charmed them all, especially her. She would never show him that.

Chef Henri walked in with their second course. It was a sandwich with a sauce on it.

"The second course is a classic Croque Monsieur with crispy fingerling potatoes."

"Chef Henri, this looks amazing. But I know you must be busy in the kitchen prepping for the dinner service tonight. You shouldn't be serving us." Louise said.

"When Monsieur Hernández requested lunch for Mademoiselle Louise, of course, I had to serve. I never get to cook for you."

"Thank you."

"Non, thank *you*." He bowed and left again.

"Your staff respects and likes you. They have given nothing but glowing reviews of your management style."

Louise felt warmth enter her cheeks and heart. She hoped that how she manages made the staff feel at home on the estate. She didn't want work to be a place that they hated.

"I'm glad." She smiled at Mr. Hernández. He smiled back again with the genuine smile that she liked.

"Dig in. Have you ever had a Croque-monsieur? It's delicious."

Mr. Hernández was right. It was the best sandwich she had in her life. It put her turkey sandwich to shame. They were quiet while enjoying this course. When the server took the dishes up, Mr. Hernández spoke up.

"I have a question for you."

"Ok…"

"Why do you insist on calling me 'Mr. Hernández' instead of Carlos?"

"Because we are professionals at work. Mr. Hernández is professional."

"You call Jamal by his first name."

"He's my cousin."

"I would need to be a relative for you to call me by my name. Or a best friend? You call Harper by her first name."

"See, that's different..."

"You also call the wait staff, the porters, the front desk clerks and almost everyone else by their first name. The only exception is Mrs. Thomas, and I suspect you still call her that because she has known you since you were a child."

There was no response from her. She couldn't tell him she called him Mr. Hernández out of spite and her stubbornness. She opened her mouth to say something but closed it again.

"See, you have no reason not to call me Carlos. And I'll call you Louise."

"But..." she tried to say.

"Carlos."

She fought against the pleasure of him saying her name. She couldn't think straight and laughed uncomfortably.

"Mr. Hernández."

This time, he rolled his eyes dramatically that made her genuinely laugh.

"I'm being professional," she lied. "I call vendors and people like that by their surname. You won't be here forever." She felt the sting of that statement. His smile faltered a little when she said it.

"Anyway, I feel like we agreed that outside of working hours, we can be more informal." She blurted.

"Do you always talk like a professor in an English class? 'Informal?'" he said.

"You bring the lecturer out of me." She smiled. He glanced at his watch. She rarely wore a watch, opting to use her phone as her time device. "What time is it?"

"Not late. We have time."

"Carlos." It slipped out, and she put her hand over her mouth. He had a 100-watt smile on his face. She liked this smile, too.

"It's 1:15." Louise jumped up. She had been without her phone for an hour, and she wanted time to prep for her meeting.

"I must go. Lunch was...enlightening." She looked over at the server. "Please give Chef Henri my compliments. And tell him I'm expecting that sandwich at least once a week."

She walked to the door and glance back at Mr. Hernández. He was watching her walk away.

CHAPTER 8

T HE REST OF the week was busy for Louise. That Friday was the estate's tree lighting ceremony. Mr. Hernández tried to coax her out of the office only one more time for lunch. But she spent much of her time making sure everything was perfect. By Friday afternoon, everything was in place and ready for that evening's activities. She felt confident enough to leave the office early to relax a little and change into her holiday spectacular outfit.

Louise got out of her work clothes and into her holiday spectacular outfit. It was faux tuxedo pants that were an ice blue with glitter down both sides. The sweater was a matching blue that hung long towards her hips. It had a snowman in various summer vacation activities around the front and back. It also had a huge sun on the shoulder that was plastic and lit up when she pressed a button. She put on three-inch white wedge boots, giving her a little height for the night. She took her hair out of its normal bun, sporting two French braids to the back that stopped at her neckline ending in two afro puffs.

After a quick dinner of some leftovers, Louise headed back to the estate. She immediately went to the ballroom. She wanted to finalize all the last-minute details. The Christmas tree was out back, but they set the ballroom up for snacks and hot cocoa for those that stayed after and needed to warm up. She was discussing the run of the night with one of the wait staff when she heard a loud whistle, then a laugh. She knew by the laugh that it was Mr. Hernández. She stifled the smile that came to her lips and turned around.

Carlos dressed casually in a pair of tight jeans and a sweater. He had a Santa hat on that made Louise giggle.

"Where did you get the hat?" she asked.

"I ran into town. You know the gift shop should sell more holiday themed clothing." He said.

"I'll put that on my list." They smiled at each other. He then looked up and down at her outfit.

"Where did you get the sweater? And the pants?" He chuckled again. He spun his finger, requesting her to turn around. She did a slow model turn and winked at him when she faced him again.

"An elf never tells her secrets."

"That won't stop me from trying."

"Try all you might, but I'm a very good elf."

"And I'm a very good secret keeper." He stepped closer and smiled down at her. Louise was happy that she had on heels that brought her height up a bit. The heels brought her a little closer to his face.

"Just because you have a Santa hat doesn't make you Santa." She reached up and grabbed the fur ball at the end of the hat. Was she flirting? Her brain was a little too muddled, and she was acting on instinct instead of her normal cautious nature. He leaned closer to her. She heard someone clear their throat. She quickly stepped back and looked at the server she had completely forgotten about.

"Thanks, sorry. That's all I need for now. I'm going to go

look outside to make sure everything is good there." The server had a sly smile as he headed back to the back doors. Louise knew that her little interaction with Mr. Hernández would be all over the estate in a few minutes. She couldn't let herself get that comfortable again. She maintained a perfect professional stance for her staff. She didn't want them to think that she was losing control.

She turned back to Mr. Hernández, who was still smiling down at her. He had her favorite smile, the turned down version of his "winning" smile. She started walking to the outer doors that lead to the back of the estate.

"I'm not sure if you had the chance to see the tree now that it's done."

"I haven't." He was walking next to her, too close. She sided stepped to break their closeness. This time, like the champ she knew she was, she did not trip. She smiled to herself; she would not be a ditzy girl from a cheesy romance novel. She wouldn't fall for the handsome stranger. Mr. Hernández reached the door before her and held it open for her to walk through, making her enter his space again, and causing her resolve from a few moments ago to falter.

"Thank you." She said and dashed away from him. She saw Jamal near the tree, and she headed in that direction.

"Hey Louise, Carlos. It's cold Lou. Where is your coat?" Jamal asked. She had forgotten her coat trying to rush out of the ballroom.

"I can go grab it for you." Carlos said. "I left mine in my room as well."

"Thanks. It's in my office." Carlos nodded and headed back to the estate. Louise took a deep breath while watching him walk away. When she looked back at Jamal, he was staring at her. He had a slight frown on his face.

"What?" she asked.

"You like him" She looked away, shaking her head. "Lou, I know you. You like him." Jamal clutched her arm. She looked back at him.

"I like him. I like everyone."

"Louise, don't make me say it." She said nothing more.

"Louise Mae Cummings, you *like* like him." They both started laughing.

"Jay, we are not in middle school anymore. Look, I'm controlling things. He will be gone soon, and we can get back to normal."

"Sweetie, I would tell you to get yours. He is cute and you're right will be gone soon. You aren't Harper. You fall hard when you fall. And it's been a long time."

Jamal was right about Louise. She was a secret romantic and romance hadn't made its way to her in a very long time. Harper and she had another big difference. Harper knew how to separate loving feelings from lusting feelings. Louise tried to be freer in college, but every guy she dated felt like he could be 'the one'. After an explosive and toxic relationship that almost derailed her master's program, she swore off men. Over the past few years, she had only been on 3 and a half dates. The half was because she left in the middle of that date.

"Nothing is going to happen."

"Sweets, it's happening." She looked away from him. He was right. The denial that she was trying to operate under was a front. She liked Carlos. She didn't know his intentions, though. She knew he was a huge flirt. He flirted with every woman in the estate so far. She tried to block out her imaginings the night that he went out with Harper. Harper didn't hook him. That doesn't mean someone else didn't. She turned back to Jamal.

"Ok, but I am in control of my feelings. You know me, so you know more than others. He won't know. I'm the one who has crushes all the time. That's all it is, a crush. Anyway, I am pretty sure he doesn't have feelings for me."

"Maybe…" She lifted her brow at him. He shrugged and pointed his chin to the door. Mr. Hernández was coming out with her coat. Jamal rested his hands on her upper arms.

"Be careful, Louise. I don't want to kill him because he broke your heart." She hugged him. Mr. Hernández made it to them. Jamal let go of her and she took her coat.

"I'm sorry to interrupt you." Mr. Hernández said.

"No interruptions, Carlos. I'm telling my favorite cousin how much I appreciate her keeping me employed." Jamal laughed and Louise pushed him.

The decorator walked up to their little group with a question for Louise. They had an hour before everything started. Louise spent the next couple of hours finishing the setup and then greeting the guests that came.

Most of the guest from the estate and most of the town would be in attendance of the tree lighting. They had a lot of activities that included a snowman-building competition, photos next to the ice sculpture, a small ice-skating pond, music, and ending with the lighting of the tree.

Louise was with Alice and her parents. They finished her photo shoot at the ice wave. The way they shaped the ice made it look like Alice and whoever took a photo in the spot shot ice from their hands. Louise was beaming as Alice gave her a big hug. The little girl was gushing the whole evening. Louise sent the family over to the pond so that the photographer could get some photos of Alice skating. Louise checked her phone. They still had an hour before they turned the tree on. She answered a few texts to her staff and looked around. She could take a little breather.

"Hello." Carlos was behind her. She closed her eyes and took a deep breath before she turned. She brought her conversation with Jamal to the forefront of her memory. He was right. A tiny part of her wished that she could have quick, hot, and fast romances. The authentic part of her knew she would fall fast for Carlos Hernández and have a broken heart in a week. As she turned, her resolve came back.

Mr. Hernández had two cups in his hands. He handed her a cup.

"I thought you must be cold. I'm freezing." She took the cup.

"No, I'm not too cold. Do you have layers on?" He shook his head. "See, that is the problem with you sunshine people. You must layer up. You have that sweater and coat, but I have on a long sleeve shirt and a thermal underwear under all this."

He nodded and shivered. They began walking as they sipped at the hot cocoa.

"Good idea to have the hot cocoa cart. For us 'sunshine' people." He laughed. "Tonight has been remarkable. You have done a great job. And you must take credit this time."

She smiled. "Thank you. I owe a lot to my decorator and her team. They brought this together. It really looks like the castle from the movie. You probably don't know the movie—"

"I do," he said. "My niece was obsessed, like every other little girl. After my brother and sister-in-law were tired of watching it with her, I got tagged in. I know way more about kiddie cartoons than I like to admit." They both laughed.

"I don't know about kiddie movies. All the younger members of our family live far away. None of my friends have kids. I'm very adult, I guess. I watched the movie a couple of more times than I will admit."

"You seem comfortable around kids."

"Yeah, in the summers we run a camp for kids and teens who have little nature experience."

"That's the charity that your father runs?"

"Yes. They started the charity about twenty years ago. We bring in disadvantaged youth for the camp. I hope that the expansion will allow for them to grow the attendees of the camp. Hopefully bring in more opportunities for growing the charity. My grandfather wanted the estate to be more than a 'hotel'."

"You have a glow whenever you talk about your work. Did you know that?" She tried not to smile, but she lost control of her face.

"I didn't know that. I love Cummings Estate. This is more than a job, it's my history. So maybe I'm a little too passionate."

"Don't say that. More people need to have a passion like you do." He gave her that warm smile that muddled her brain.

"What about you? Are you passionate about your job?" He looked away, his smile fading.

"I like my job. It pays the bills." They walked in silence for a bit. She noticed they weren't going in a certain direction.

"What can you do to be passionate about your job?" she asked. He stopped walking. She turned and looked at him. He was looking off in the distance with a frown. "I'm sorry. I'm not usually this nosy."

He looked at her and gave her the 'winning' smile.

"Don't apologize." He started walking again. Louise felt something shift between them. That 'winning' smile always felt like a mask to her. She was being open with him, but he closed the door. This made her close her own door. She looked at her phone. It was 30 minutes until the tree lighting. They were walking away from the tree. She stopped and headed back in that direction.

As she walked, she didn't feel him next to her. She wanted to look back to find him, but she wouldn't let her neck turn. The cold felt colder now that she didn't have his warmth beside her. She heard him laughing as she got further away. It mingled with a feminine laugh. She knew he wasn't alone. She tried to stifle the hurt that laugh caused.

CHAPTER 9

W HEN IT WAS time for the tree to be lit, Jamal was on their little stage with Alice's family. Louise made sure that Jamal would oversee all the speeches. She joked about him being a ham, but he was the entertainer of the family. He had a degree in theater arts and lead the entertainment in town. Louise had found her parents, and they were all standing to the side of the stage. They had a switch that Alice would hit to turn on the tree.

She was facing the crowd, so this time she saw Mr. Hernández as he walked up. The assistant chef was by his side. She frowned. He caught the frown before she could put her plastic smile on. She looked away from him to Jamal and Alice. Jamal had the crowd count down before Alice hit the switch.

The tree was more beautiful than she planned. There was a hush in the crown before they erupted in applause and shouts. The Fraser fir tree was about 20 feet tall. They decorated the branches in ice blue, white, and silver ornaments ranging from small to some the size of basketballs. The lights were white with twinkling blue. Jamal brought the decorator and her team up and thanked them on behalf of the estate.

Louise's smile was genuine again as she saw the faces of Alice and her parents. She looked around the crowd, who were still excitedly clapping and in awe. She tried to stop her eyes from roaming to the spot she last saw Mr. Hernández. Her eyes were being rebellious. He still stood there, this time with the smile she knew as her smile. He nodded at her as he clapped in her direction. She tipped her head to him. He walked up to her.

"Wow." He said. She turned back to the tree. Her door was closed, she told her brain.

"It's pretty amazing." She said over her shoulder.

"You're pretty amazing." She thought she heard him say, but her father started talking at the same time.

"Baby girl! You out did yourself this year." Her father gave her a big bear hug that lifted her off her feet. Her mom was right here hugging as soon as dad let go. When her mom let go, she looked up at Mr. Hernández.

"Mom, Dad, this is Mr. Hernández. Mr. Hernández, this is my mom and dad." She tried to ignore the look that Carlos gave her.

"Carlos, please," he said as he shook Louise's parents' hands. "It's nice to meet you, Mr. and Mrs. Cummings."

"It's nice to meet you finally, young man." Her father said as he clapped Carlos on the shoulder. "I have been wanting to meet you, but today has been my first day at the estate this season. Louise, do you mind if I talk to Carlos for a while?"

She shook her head, but she minded. She minded a lot. They walked off without her, and she was not happy about it. She wanted to know what her father had to say. She followed, but her mom stopped her.

"Let the men talk, Lou. You forgot to mention how attractive he was."

"Mom," she rolled her eyes. "Let's go over there."

"Louise, your father wants to ask some questions. He doesn't need you eavesdropping." Her mother hooked her arm and walked them in the opposite direction.

"So, is he single?" her mom asked. Louise shrugged, not wanting to engage in this conversation.

"He is adorable enough. You should find out if he is single. The way he was looking at you." She looked at her mother, who had a sly smile on her face.

"What are you talking about? He wasn't looking at me any kind of way."

"I see things, honey. When he was in the crowd, his eyes left you only to look at the tree for a second." Louise vigorously shook her head. She did not need this information in her head. She closed the door. Her mother had to be mistaken.

"Mom..."

"I'm just saying. Anyway, the tree and everything looks amazing." Louise was so glad her mother changed the subject.

"Thanks. I had so much help. But I think this is the best the estate looked during the holidays. At least since I took over."

"You are right. It's the best it's been. I'm proud of you, baby." Louise's mom smile at her.

They heard Jamal announcing that the ballroom was now open for light snacks. Louise and her mother headed to the ballroom doors. In the ballroom, Louise got busy helping the staff restock and serve. The crowd was bigger than she had expected. She was excited, but it kept her and the staff busy well into the wee hours of the night. Around 2 a.m., the last of the crowd had finally left. She felt exhaustion down to her pinkie toes as they finish the last of the kitchen cleanup. She went to the ballroom and sent the last of the waitstaff home. They could finish clean-up in the morning.

As she headed to her office to grab her purse, she saw Carlos at the front desk with Harper. Harper was showing him something on the computer. They looked up when they heard her getting closer. Carlos gave her the smile she loved. She looked away before her face matched his.

"Grabbing my purse. Carry on, you two." She continued walking to the offices, but Carlos was by her side in seconds.

"Harper was showing me the booking and reservations programs."

"Um, huh." She nodded. She then pulled out her phone to check over her notifications. There were a lot of notification tagging the estate on social media. She smiled. Hopefully, this would put them on Top Ten lists of holiday destinations. She made it to her office and grabbed her purse. She turned and Carlos was standing in the doorway.

"What's up Carlos?" He smirked at her.

"I'm glad we didn't take steps backwards." She walked past him.

"I thought you would be in bed hours ago."

"I wanted to see the cleanup process. You were washing dishes."

"It was a big job. I help where I'm needed."

"I want you to know that you had me do a thing I promised myself I would never do again." She looked up at him quizzically. "I'd promise myself after my last serving job I would never bus a table again. I saw you and Jamal helping, so I couldn't just stand there."

She laughed. His golden eyes were warm and melting. They were wrenching her door back open. She turned away from him.

"Thank you for your help." They made it to the front desk. She waved goodnight to Harper, then turned to wave at Carlos.

"No," he said, "I'm walking to your front door. It's the middle of the night."

"That's ok. I'll be fine."

"I'm walking to your door." He said that with a firmness she hadn't heard from him before.

"Ok." She looked at Harper, whose mouth was partly open. Harper wouldn't be of any help, as she seemed to enjoy the show. Louise knew her phone would blow up in five minutes. Carlos was waiting for her at the door, so she followed him out.

They were quiet as they walked down the path. Carlos was very close to Louise. So close that their hands brushed against each other. Louis quickly crossed her arms before she could grab his hand.

"Are you cold?" He asked.

"No. Just tired."

"I want to say again, you did an amazing job. The estate looks magical. I sent pictures to my niece. She is very jealous. I wish I can fly them up here."

"That would be nice."

"It would be nice. I live in the same city as my family, but only see them about once or twice a month."

"I understand that. I rarely go to town. I get everything I need delivered. Or I can grab it from the store in the estate."

"Sounds like we both need to learn some work/life balance." They made it to her door. She smiled up at him.

"You are probably right. Thanks for walking me to my door."

"You are welcome." They both stared at each other. Louise couldn't stop herself from looking at his lips. They were full and kissable. She reached in her purse for her keys, still looking at his face. He stepped in closer, and she caught her breath. She leaned into him and looked back into his eyes. He grabbed the keys from her hand and unlocked the door for her. Then he opened it.

"You better get inside. Get some rest." She was overwhelmed and a little disappointed that he didn't kiss her. But she couldn't kiss him. She couldn't even think of him like that. She looked at him and smiled. He didn't smile, but his stare was deep. She couldn't read his face. She went into the house, closing the door.

"Sleep well Louise." He said.

"You too, Carlos." She let his name roll off her tongue. He would be back to Mr. Hernández in the morning. His smile, the one she claimed as her own, came back as she shut the door.

CHAPTER 10

T HE NEXT MORNING, Louise was all smiles as she did
her daily routine. She couldn't get the sight of Carlos's
smile out of her mind. But as she made the walk to the
estate, reality set in. Her nerves were on edge as she thought
about how to approach Carlos today. The night before was such
a roller-coaster of emotions. At the forefront was the smile and
the almost kiss she wanted to happen, she told herself. He leaned
in to be nice. He was being a gentleman.

Louise shook her head before entering the building. Everything
from the night before had to be locked up tight into the deepest,
darkest corner of her brain. Today wouldn't be an extremely busy
day, but she needed to manage getting the ballroom cleaned up
and planning for their annual Christmas eve ball. She also had
a lot of paperwork she needed to get to that she put to the side
all week. People needed her signature on purchasing orders. She
was a busy person. She didn't have time to think about warm
honey eyes and soft, kissable lips.

When she walked in, instead of her routine of looking at the
ceiling, she looked directly at his chair. It was empty for the first

time in two weeks. She looked over at the front desk. Harper was talking to the front desk person who would relieve her.

"Good morning, Lou."

"Good morning." She tried to sound cheery, but even she could hear the disappointment in her voice.

"Don't look so sad. He's already in your office. He has a surprise." It took the strength of 10 bodybuilders for her not to smile or react to Harper's statement. Harper left the desk and walked up to Louise.

"You need to respond to my text messages. What happened last night? I fully expected not to see him back so soon. Why didn't you invite him in for coffee or a drink or something?" Harper whispered.

"Harper, I have to work. This is not the time." She left Harper standing there with her arms crossed. Louise took a few more deep breaths before entering her office. She could smell the coffee before she entered the room.

Carlos was sitting in his seat when she entered. His head was bent over his computer. She noticed that his hair was a little longer than the day he walked into her life. Today the curls glistened, still damp from his shower this morning. She wanted to run her hands through those curls for hours. After two minutes, she finally looked around the room. On her side of the desk was an enormous platter with a top.

"Good morning, Mr. Hernández." She had way more bass in her voice than she intended, making her sound very sultry. She cleared her throat as he turned to her. "How are you doing this morning?"

"I'm doing amazing. And if you say 'Mr. Hernández' like that again you can call me that forever."

She tried to laugh off his comment. This conversation started off wrong. She floundered, trying to steer the conversation back to a professional one, ignoring his comment and his sexy, sly smile. She wanted to claim that smile as her own.

"What's this?" she gestured to the platter as she sat and put her things away.

"I knew you would be here at 6:30 a.m. sharp, even though you couldn't have gotten much sleep. So, I had us some snacks brought in." He stood and removed the top. The platter was full of the most delectable pastries she had ever seen.

"If you ever ate breakfast in the dining room, you would get to enjoy these yourself. You know your pastry chef is amazing."

"All of my staff is amazing. But these are perfection." She took the pastry the closest to her and took a bite. As she chewed, she closed her eyes and moaned. She leaned back in her chair and took another bite. After a few seconds, she remembered Mr. Hernández. He was staring at her with something in his eyes that caused her stomach to tighten. She sat up quickly and put the pastry down.

"This is not good for my diet."

"Don't worry about your diet. You shouldn't be on a diet, anyway. You look great." His eyes lowered as much as he could see. She was glad to be sitting where the desk obscured his view. She couldn't handle his eyes roaming her body. After clearing her throat, she turned on her computer.

"What's on the schedule for today?" he asked with a smile still in his voice. Good, they needed to focus on work.

"Today is a typical Saturday. I have a lot of paperwork to catch up on. I put off a few things for the tree lighting."

"Good. I have some suggestions about your paperwork process." She looked at him, all humor draining from her.

"Excuse me?"

"I've noticed that when it comes to any paperwork, you must read through it. You sign off on all purchasing orders, and, like this week, things are on hold waiting for you."

"I'm the manager. What, do you want me to let everyone do what they want?"

"I'm not saying that. I'm saying that you could delegate more responsibility to Jamal. He is your assistant manager. He could have handled some of that paperwork this week."

"Jamal is busy with his own duties."

"Yes, many of those duties deal with things outside of running the actual estate. He is very busy with the charity and things in town. He has found other tasks because you don't let him do anything here."

Louise stood angrier than she ever been.

"Excuse me?" He held his hands up.

"I'm giving you my observations. Also, I went over the program you all used to make reservations. It is very antiquated. Harper showed me how the estate almost got over booked this season. If it wasn't for the rooms you usually hold to the side, you would have had some upset clients."

She didn't have words; she was so upset. She stood there, opening and closing her mouth.

"Please sit down, Ms. Cummings." She was too shocked to do anything else. She felt ice climbing her veins, especially the way he said her name.

"I'm sorry for the bluntness, but I came here to consult. I spent the past couple of weeks observing, and now it's time to present my observations."

He moved the platter of pastries to a side table. He then put a packet in front of her.

"This is the report I compiled. I have also emailed it to you, Jamal, and the board. If you are ready, we can go over it."

For the next few hours, Mr. Hernández went through every single detail of running the estate. The report he presented to Louise was thorough. He highlighted the things they were doing well. He also pointed out the places where they were lacking with an accuracy that made Louise cringe. *He's good at his job.* This information would have thrilled her if aimed at another business. She wouldn't be able to treat him like a lover boy and a flirt. He was detailed and focused.

By the end of the day, she had a major headache and ground her teeth. She was full of fury towards this man that had completely disrupted her life. She had every plan to work on the things in the estate that could improve. She had lists with tasks of improvements over the next year. To see all of it in front of her face fired up the insecurities that she held at bay ever since she took over as manager. She knew that her family, most of them at least, trusted her judgment, but she still felt insecure.

Louise spent eight years in school, had a master's degree, and still felt like a child in the business. She wanted to ball up and cry but couldn't because Mr. Hernández kept talking and looking at her. She refused to show her weakness to the man that spent the past two weeks fattening her up for this slaughter.

"I think that is enough for today." He said as he packed up his stuff. "Louise, I..."

"Ms. Cummings, please."

He nodded. She looked at him and he seemed to realize that the friendliness they had built was gone.

"Ms. Cummings, please don't take this as a reflection of your management. Some of these issues go back years before you took the role. I feel that if you take the time to address these items now, the expansion that you are planning will be more successful than you can imagine."

He attempted a small smile. It was the first time she sensed him being unsure. She didn't respond to the smile. She was angry and hurt and even more frustrated with herself because she allowed the hurt. Mr. Hernández was doing his job. That shouldn't hurt her. But she was hurt. She lowered her head. She heard him open the door and close it back. She looked up at the empty room. She felt the pressure behind her eyes but couldn't figure out if the tears were for Cummings' estate or her heart.

THAT EVENING, LOUISE cleaned her already clean house to work off her frustration. She was in her kitchen, wiping out the cabinets. She had pulled everything out and was reorganizing her kitchen. She had paid for an online order of kitchen gadgets that she didn't need, but shopping and cleaning were her go-to destressors.

As she finished putting the last of her dishes back in the cabinet, she heard her door camera ring. She took a deep breath. She was annoyed to think it might be Mr. Hernández. It excited the small but loud voice at the back of her head at the thought of him in her home. She checked her phone, and the camera showed Harper, not Mr. Hernández.

Louise went to the door to let Harper in. Harper had a brown bag in her hand. She reached in and pulled out a bottle of tequila. A bottle of good, expensive tequila.

"I heard you had a hard day." Harper's comment was an under-statement.

After Mr. Hernández left, Louise allowed herself to cry behind her closed door. She wasn't noisy, but Jamal was at her door five minutes later and held her hand as she let the last of her tears come out. He had read the report and was disappointed, too. He tried to comfort her reminding her that some of those issues they had discussed before. They were issues the estate dealt with for years. They spent an hour talking and griping about the report. He could even lift her mood a little. But by the time Louise made it home, her sadness turned back to anger.

Louise took the bottle from Harper, nodded, and headed to her China cabinet for shot glasses. They settled at her dining room table with the limes Harper also brought.

"You know I haven't had tequila since college." Louise said.

Harper poured the first two shots.

"Not since that time I came down for that weekend?" Harper asked.

"That is the exact moment," Louise laughed. "I swore I would never drink a drop of alcohol after that. You are a bad influence on me."

"But did you die?" Harper started laughing. They both took their shot. Harper poured two more shots. "What happened? Jamal didn't say much. He said today was rough."

Louise gave Harper the abridged version of the day. Harper whistled.

"How do you feel about it?" She asked.

"I'm mad, of course. A little disappointed. And really pissed at myself. I fell into this familiar relationship with him. We were being friendly. Anyway, I should have remembered that he is here for a job, nothing else."

"I'm sorry, Lou." Harper held Louise's hand. "And I wasn't any help, trying to push you both together. Well, from now on, he is on our hit list."

Louise smiled. Harper would always have her back. Harper pulled her tablet out of her bag. "Let's call Angie. I told her to get some tequila, too. If we are going to drink, we are going to do it right."

Harper called Angie, and they all took another shot. Louise's best friends brought her out of her funk. They helped her to verbalize her feelings. They were non-judgmental and supportive, and Louise needed to get the past two weeks off her chest. Angie, the wise one, left her with a piece of advice that she would chew on.

"Lou, even though it turned out differently than you expected, it's nice that you had these feelings for him. You deserve love. You deserve to be treated well by a man you like. Just because Carlos Hernández is not the one doesn't mean the one isn't out there. You must stop locking yourself up on that estate. Love, you aren't Sleeping Beauty."

Louise knew Angie was right. The story books never mentioned how Sleeping Beauty was supposed to wake herself up.

CHAPTER 11

LOUISE WOKE THE next day slightly hungover. It was later than 6:30. She gave herself an hour to relax and change into work clothes. She also needed time for the aspirin to work. Mr. Hernández can wait. That is the least he deserved.

When she made it to the estate, Mr. Hernández wasn't sitting in his chair. Louise went straight to her office, and it was empty. On her desk was a bag and a note. She opened the bag first. It was the Danish she liked from the day before. She then opened the note.

I thought you could use a day off from me and my report.
Enjoy the pastry.
- Carlos

He was right. Louise could use a break from him and that report. But her disappointment was a huge rock in the pit of her stomach.

The rest of the day was quiet for Louise. She completed her paperwork, and no one bothered her all day long. She took a few breaks from her office to roam around the lobby. She told herself that it was because she needed to stretch her legs. She didn't see Mr. Hernández in any of her walks. Maybe he was hiding out in his room or hanging in town. Wait a minute—it didn't matter where he was or what he was doing.

When she woke on Monday, she had no idea what to expect from the day. It had been more than twenty-four hours since the last time she saw Mr. Hernández. Their last meeting was contentious. She was still mad, but the strongest part of her rage was gone. And under her anger hung that fact that she missed him. Her office felt lonely. She didn't know how she was going to get back to normal after he left.

She walked through the front doors and looked up at the ceiling art. She needed to draw on the strength she gained from those intricate designs. Closing her eyes, she took a breath before looking. He was there; she was relieved. He had a hesitant smile on his face that made him look more vulnerable than she had ever seen him.

"Good morning." She said.

"Good morning."

She started walking towards her office but didn't feel him follow. She looked back, and he was still sitting, staring at her. His smile faded.

"I wasn't sure if you wanted to see me today." He said. Louise looked over at the front desk person who hands looked busy, but she could tell they were listening to every word. She would have to ask Harper what the estate's gossips were talking about.

"We can talk in my office." She turned back in her original direction and walked away. He was at her door before her opening it for her. She walked in and got settled at her desk. Mr. Hernández hovered at the door. She cleared her throat.

"Saturday was . . . difficult. You weren't done, so we had better get this over with." She looked up at him with more venom in her eyes. "The sooner we finish this, the sooner you can leave."

Louise saw his pained look. He took a deep breath and then walked to his chair. *Her chair*, she reminded herself. That was *her* chair, and this was *her* office, not theirs. She decided to get a new chair when he left.

He still looked hurt by her remark. He nodded and fixed his face into a casual grin. She knew his face too well to think it was casual. It was a terrible mask. He pulled out his computer, and she pulled out the report. They started on the page they left off.

The rest of the morning went better than Saturday. She was more open to listening to the report now that her initial rage had settled. She tried not to take his words as a direct hit to her ego. As he said a few times already, this was to improve the estate.

Around lunch, he stood and stretched.

"I could use a break. I'm sure you could too. Will you join me for lunch?" he said. She looked at him. There was hope in his eyes. She wanted to go, and she wanted to stay. She opened her mouth, still not sure of her answer, when there was a knock on the door. Jamal peeked around the door when she told him to come in.

"Is everything good in here? You both have been quiet all morning." Jamal asked.

"We were about to take a break for lunch." Mr. Hernández said. "I was trying to convince Ms. Cummings to join me."

Both men looked at her for her answer. She flicked her eyes to Jamal, then back to Mr. Hernández. She was still stuck in indecision. Jamal spoke up, to her relief.

"Did you forget, Lou, you promised to show me that thing? I already ordered lunch for us."

Mr. Hernández looked back and forth between them. She could read the disappointment on his face. At that moment, all the anger melted away. She spent the morning trying to hurt him, and she was successful. Now she was sad and felt sorry for him. She looked to Jamal and nodded. Mr. Hernández left her office.

Jamal and Louise settled into his office. She waited while he'd officially ordered them some lunch. Her usual turkey sandwich and a fruit bowl. They were silent while they waited. When the food arrived, Louise didn't have an appetite to eat.

"I ordered this old sad sandwich for you, and you aren't going to eat it?" Jamal asked. She gave him a weak smile.

"I'm not hungry." She looked at the food. Jamal handed her the fruit bowl.

"Eat something. Was today as bad as Saturday?"

"No. It's better, actually. He is right about The Cummings. But you said that already."

"Then…"

"I have been taking jabs all morning at him. He just took it. No response and then asked me to lunch. I'm horrible." Louise put her head on Jamal's desk.

"You aren't horrible. At your meanest, you are still like a cartoon character." She looked up at him. Jamal was smiling. "You are like a cute Helga."

Louise shook her head and laughed at the reference to *Hey Arnold!*, their favorite cartoon show when they were kids.

"So, you are saying I've been so mean because I am obsessed with Mr. Hernández?"

"You have every right to be upset. You are protective of Cummings. But I think the sting is because you like him."

Louise sat back in her chair. Jamal was right. Her anger was stronger because she was falling for him. She had to get back to her professional side with him. For real this time.

"You are right, of course. I guess I need to apologize. I've decided that I need to get back to me." Jamal's eyebrow raised.

She laughed, then explained. "I was overly professional at first, then I was under professional. I'm going back to my normal self around him. I will treat him like any of my co-workers. Be friendly but with an air of professionalism. That should make the next few days go smoothly and then we will be done, and he will be back on a flight to his home."

She nodded to herself at her plan. Jamal still looked skeptical.

"What?" she asked.

"Nothing."

"Jamal, go ahead. You don't curb your tongue any other time."

"Lou, I have nothing to say. I'm going to see how this plays out."

"Good to know my life can offer you a little entertainment." She got up, took her sandwich and fruit, and walked back to her office. She would be hungry later. Mr. Hernández hadn't returned.

Louise settled into her desk and breathed through her next task. She would need to clear the air between her and Mr. Hernández so that they could get back to a professional relationship. A few minutes later he finally walked back in. He didn't look at her while he sat and woke up his computer.

Louise cleared her throat to get his attention. He finally looked up with a weary expression. She tried to smile, but it looked more like a grimace. She shook her head and began.

"I, um...I owe you an apology. I'm sorry." He looked confused. "I haven't reacted well today. Or the other day. I have been unnecessarily mean. I'm sorry about that. While you were observing the estate, I became comfortable with how we interacted. So, I got angry when you presented your findings. I took it personally. I shouldn't have. Like you, Jamal, and my friends all said, you are just doing your job. You did a great job. You are good at your job. You pulled out all the pressure points Jamal and I reviewed over a million times. I hoped I was doing a good enough job that others couldn't see them." He began to speak, but Louise held up her hand to stop him.

"I heard you. You are right, if we want to achieve the success we want for the estate, we must address these issues. Your job was to consult, and this report shows that we have some things to take care of." She couldn't read his expression. *That was good,* she thought to herself. After all, she didn't really know this man.

"Thank you." He sat back and thought. Louise waited, watching him. "I didn't want to hurt you. The report was one part of my job. The part I dislike. Your reaction wasn't different from other businesses I consulted for." He leaned to her and put his hand on her desk. "But you have done so many amazing things. I put those in the report too."

She nodded, and a small smile came to her. "I noticed those, too. But I couldn't see past the anger at first. I appreciate that. This," she motioned to the report, "brought up all my insecurities of being the manager." She sucked in a breath. She didn't mean to say that.

Mr. Hernández covered her hand. She hated that her body reacted to that small touch. She told herself to pull back, but she didn't.

"You are a brilliant manager. You are what the Cummings estate needs. Don't doubt that." His eyes were so intense that she couldn't look away. They stayed like that for what seemed like hours. He finally let go of her hand and straightened up. She did the same and aimlessly moved things around on her desk. He went to his bag and pulled out a new packet. He handed it to her, but she didn't take it.

"I know you want nothing else from me, but please take it." She finally took it and skimmed over the first few pages.

"What is this?" she asked, her brows furrowed.

"Now that we talked about some of your pressure points at Cummings Estate, it's time we talk about how to relieve that pressure."

She looked at the first idea and smiled. It was a suggestion of ways to incorporate a new reservation system. She hated the system that was used to book the guest online and was looking at some new tools. The suggestion that Mr. Hernández had would work and not be too costly.

"You probably won't like all the ideas, that's ok. I want us to work together to come up with a plan that will work for the Cummings." She nodded as he talked, and she dug deeper into the suggestions.

"I also think now we need to bring Jamal into our meetings. A lot of what I put will have you working on extensive projects, so you will have to delegate better. You have a great staff you trust. Now it's time to show them that."

Louise looked up at him, knowing he was right. She struggled to relinquish control. She didn't want to think of herself as controlling, but she also didn't want that blame to be placed on anyone other than herself if something went wrong. If she took all the blame, then she also needed to make sure nothing went wrong. The smile that she loved was back. He seemed to have relaxed again.

"Ok, Carlos Hernández. Now shut up so I can read this thing." She didn't miss the sparkle that hit his eyes as she said his full name.

CHAPTER 12

FOR THE NEXT couple of days, Louise, Jamal, and Carlos (Mr. Hernández) sat in the small conference room and hashed out the plan to support The Cummings Estate. Louise kept her temper at bay, but sometimes it was still contentious. She liked a few of Mr. Hernández's ideas, but the rest didn't fit into what she envisioned for Cummings. Carlos was very confident in his ideas, causing friction between the two. Louise was happy that Jamal was there to be a buffer and a voice of reason for them both.

One issue of contention was the suggestion that Mr. Hernández made to hire additional staff. Cummings Estate management always consisted of family or highly trusted staff. They rarely hired management from outside of the estate. Chef Henri was the only one hired from the outside, but he also came with many awards and a promise to help the Cummings Estate. But hiring him came with a lot of back and forth with the board. When Mr. Hernández suggested hiring a supervisor of Guest services and a new marketing firm, Louise strongly disagreed.

"No!" Jamal and Mr. Hernández looked at her. Mr. Hernández put his head in his hands. Not for the first time.

"Lou, come on. Just hear him out... *again.*" Louise could hear the frustration in Jamal's voice.

"Hear what out? Jamal, you and I both know how the board will react." She turned to Mr. Hernández, who still had his face covered. "Mr. Hernández as I have explained, the board will not agree to hiring another supervisor. It doesn't matter, anyway; I am doing fine with managing staff. I don't need another manager."

"And as I have explained, *Ms. Cummings*, you want to build another hotel and cabins. You cannot support the hiring of all that staff, keep up with the demands of this estate and managing everything else you currently manage. Something will have to give. Creating this position will lesson your load."

"You don't think I can do my job?" She stood up in a huff and walked to where they had snacks and drinks.

"Lou, this has nothing to do with how Carlos feels about how you do your job. Get out of your feelings!"

Louise turned, giving Jamal a death glare. He shrugged but didn't wilt under her stare. They stayed in that death stare for a beat.

"Ms. Cummings?" Louise finally looked back at Mr. Hernández. "I know you can handle a lot. You have done a great job. But you want to expand. You won't be able to create this dream alone. We can handle the board together. But I need you to know that Jamal and I believe in your abilities. We know what you can do. You don't have to do it by yourself."

Louise turned back to the snacks. She grabbed a bottle of water and poured it into a cup. *Breathe, Louise. Deep cleansing breaths*, she kept saying to herself, overwhelmed by the emotion that Mr. Hernández's words caused. She knew that her family believed in her, but she couldn't stop putting the pressure to do it all on herself.

Louise finally turned back to the table. Mr. Hernández had an encouraging smile on his face. His eyes were warm, and she settled in them for a second. She nodded to him, then returned to her seat.

"I'm sorry, Jay." Jamal nodded but still looked weary. "Ok, explain it one more time."

"I'm proposing you hire a supervisor for guest services. They will oversee staffing and work with the housekeeping and kitchen managers for their hiring/firing. This will take a lot off your plate. When the new property opens, this will allow you to focus over there. In the restructuring, you will be the general manager for both properties, with Jamal taking over as manager here. Eventually, you can hire similar staff at the new property," said Carlos.

Louise let the suggestions roll over her brain. She wanted to give Jamal more responsibility. He gave as much time and effort to Cummings as she did and deserved to be more of a leader. It all made a sense to her. She had to be honest with herself—pride was the only thing holding her back.

She looked over at Jamal before she began. "Ok, you both are right. Jamal?"

The weary look was still there.

"Jamal, I'm sorry." He waved her away, the hint of a smile forming.

"This is a good idea. I need to let go, a little. Carlos, let's put it in the report." Louise saw the excited shock come to his face as she slipped. She couldn't help but to laugh internally as she causally used his first name as if he would be here forever.

"This marketing thing will not work." Both Carlos and Jamal groaned. "I get that a larger firm could get us more attention, but we have been with Myer's Firm for years. Yes, they are small, but I also don't want to be a small fish in a large pond with this firm you suggested, Carlos."

Louise opened the Carlos gates, and she wouldn't be able to close them. He smiled her smile while shaking his head.

"I agree with Louise." Jamal said. "My dad hired a larger firm a few years ago. We got lost in that firm. They tried to market us as something we weren't. The Myer's Firm knows us. They understand we are a family-owned and operated estate and that we want our guests to feel like family. We don't want the same thing to happen if we go to a bigger firm."

"Ok," Carlos nodded, "I understand. What if I find a larger firm, not too large, that has a family feel but more resources? I think the Myer's firm has done an excellent job with your marketing, but it's time to go bigger. They may not have the resources to put you on those Top 10 Lists that Louise keeps hoping for.

"If you get some names, we will investigate it. We can talk to them." Louise said.

"I will also talk to Roger. Maybe they can work with another firm to expand our marketing." Jamal said.

"Good!" Carlos clapped his hands together once. "Let's get this down before she changes her mind again." He directed that to Jamal, but Louise heard the playful lift in his voice. She smiled at him. It was nice that the tension finally broke.

By Friday afternoon, they finally had a plan that they all felt comfortable about presenting to the board. Louise was more than comfortable; she was proud of the plan they spent all week coming up with. They incorporated how the expansion, if approved, could work with the strategies. Louise was sitting in her office reading over the report one last time before sending it out.

Carlos was back in his room. They all needed a break from the long week. Louise was glad to be alone to write the email.

She smiled to herself as she composed it and hit send. She sat back in her seat. Although she was initially angry that the board voted to bring in Carlos Hernández's firm, she now was glad that they did. Carlos ended up being what Louise needed to see beyond her own reasoning. She needed an outside voice that saw the vision but also could see the pitfalls. She believed that with the help Carlos gave, the estate will be successful over the next few years.

Louise even had the idea to keep his company on retainer for future consults. She composed a quick email to Jamal about the idea and told him he should lead this project. Breathe, let go, and delegate.

Someone knocked on Louise's door and a smile came to her face. She told the knocker to come in, but it wasn't Carlos, it was Harper.

"Did you expect someone else?" Harper asked. Louise's smile didn't change. At least she hoped it didn't when Harper came in.

"No, I'm happy to see you. How are you?"

"I'm good. I haven't seen you all week! I missed you. You haven't texted us back."

"I missed you too." Louise grabbed her phone. She turned back on the notifications. She had her phone on focus all week, so she missed a lot. "We had a long week."

"I saw Jamal leaving. He looked exhausted. But he said that it went well."

"It did. I'm elated."

"This is definitely better than the last time I saw you." They both laughed. Louise released a deep breath, leaning back in her chair.

"I'm glad you are relaxed!" Harper said. "We have a surprise for you."

"What surprise?"

"The best surprise ever!" Angie ran into her office and screamed. Louise jumped up and all three of them hugged. Angela Cho, the third member of the Three Musketeers, as their parents called them, was the median between Harper's free and flowing attitude and Louise's all-business demeanor. She was taller than Louise but shorter than Harper, right in the middle, as usual. She wore her black hair in a chin-length bob, her fair skin adorned with a small amount of makeup. She wore name-brand clothes from the Hermes scarf around her head down to her Prada flats.

Angie broke the embrace and smiled at Louise. "I came up early for the holiday. After last week, I thought you could use a little more reinforcement."

"Ang, you didn't have to do that, but I'm glad you did." Louise laughed. "Especially since everything is wonderful now."

"I heard. So, when do I get to meet *him*? I'm tired of Harper's descriptions."

Louise rolled her eyes and went to her desk to grab her things. "You can meet him tomorrow. But now let's go to my house. I want to celebrate. Are you staying with your parents?"

"I was hoping I didn't have to." Angie said.

"You can stay with me." They all hugged again, then headed to Louise's house.

CHAPTER 13

L ATER, THEY ALL settled at Louise's dining room table. She made them dinner, and they spent time catching up. "This feels right. I know you are successful in Atlanta, but I want you to move back, Ang." Harper said. "I don't like us being so far away."

"If I moved back, you would leave. Your art will blow up any second now and you will be in L. A. or Paris." Harper sighed. Louise wished she had the confidence in her work that way that everyone else did.

"Whatever. We need to celebrate you being home early and Louise's happy week."

"We are celebrating." Louise said. "I cooked. Anyway, the week wasn't all happy, it just ended happy. Now I need to wait until the board has time to read through the recommendations."

"Thank you for cooking, but I mean a proper celebration." Harper's eyes lit up. She looked over at Angie and winked.

"What do you two have planned?" Louise asked.

"Look, Louise Cummings, you are going out with your best friends. And I don't want to hear your mouth or excuses!" Harper said.

"We are getting Sleeping Beauty out!" Angie added. Louise shook her head, but they each clasped an arm and took her to her bedroom. Harper started going through her closet.

"Now let's find her something worth wearing. Louise! Why so many Christmas sweaters?" Harper asked. Angie went to the guest room and came back with a shopping bag.

"Good thing I thought ahead." She gave the bag to Louise. It was from a plus-sized clothing store that was far from the area. Louise had gone to the store and loved their clothing while in Atlanta visiting Angie a couple of years ago. She pulled out a faux leather mini shirt, a couple of pairs of jeans, and a couple of tops.

"Angie! This is too much. I must pay you back."

"Merry Christmas! Consider this your Christmas and birthday gifts. I hope everything fits. My shopper still has both of your sizes from our trip last year." Harper was already going through the clothes, making an outfit for Louise.

"What did you bring me?" Harper asked. Angie pushed her and pointed to the door.

"It's in my bag, but you can't have it until Christmas Day. So, what is she going to wear?"

Harper held up the skirt and a green, long sleeve top with a deep V-neck. Louise shook her head. Harper ran out of the room.

"It's still wintertime. I can't wear that, I'll catch cold." Harper came running back in the room with knee high stiletto boots.

"I'm glad I bought these. Now change. I told you we don't want to hear your mouth. You are going out and that's that."

Over the next hour, the ladies got dress and did each other make-up. Harper and Angie did Louise's makeup, as Louise usually only wore lipstick. They kept it simple by giving her a smoky, winged look and light foundation. Louise looked in the mirror and approved. She was happy to have her friends together. They hadn't spent time like this in a while. They only saw each other during the holidays and took at least one girl's trip a year. FaceTiming and texts weren't the same as the in-person quality time Louise craved.

When they finished getting ready, they admired themselves in Louise's full-length mirror. Harper had brought a bag to spend the weekend at Louise's, too. Louise was a little jealous that Harper got away with wearing jeans; tightly fitted jeans, and a low-cut red top. Angie had on leggings and a long, backless silver top. Louise wanted some pants. She convinced her friends to let her wear some tights under the super short skirt.

Angie took the wheel of Louise's car as the designated driver. They drove to a nearby town that had a large nightclub. As soon as they got to the club, Harper pulled both friends out on the dance floor. They spent a couple of songs dancing. Louise really loosened up. She hadn't been out dancing in a couple of years. The music took her away.

Louise pulled the ladies to the bar and bought the first round of drinks. They found an empty table and sat listening to the music. Harper perked up, seeing someone near the door.

"Be right back!" she yelled over the music. A few minutes later, she came back with Jamal and Silas in tow. Louise jumped up and hugged them both.

"What did she do to get the old married couple out?" Louise asked. Jamal rolled his eyes, but Silas was excited. Louise's stomach settled back in. She was terrified who Harper would return with.

"She talked to Si instead of me. I was in bed reading a good book when he dragged me out of the house."

"And was it worth it?" Silas said as he looked Louise up and down. "You look beautiful. Come on." Silas grasped Louise's hand and took her to the dance floor. Soon, Jamal and Angie joined them.

LOUISE AND ANGIE came from the lady's room. Louise wanted to wipe off some of the sweat that accumulated from all her dancing. She also checked her hair. She wanted to make sure her braid out still looked somewhat controlled. With her hair and make-up fresh, Louise was ready to hit the dance floor again. Angie steered them to the bar where she saw Jamal and Silas talking to a tall stranger. Louise froze. The stranger they were talking to was not a stranger. It was Carlos Hernández.

"Don't kill me." Harper whispered in her ear. Louise whipped her head behind her to where Harper stood. She had a sly smile.

"What?" asked Angie. Harper pointed, and Angie inhaled deeply. Jamal stepped over and the fullness of Carlos Hernández was visible to them. He had on a form fitting button-down shirt with the top two buttons open. A pair of grey pants that fit his form so well. Louise felt her mouth open and looked over at Angie, whose mouth was also open. Louise tried to take a step back, but Harper was there and pushing her forward.

Carlos looked in their direction and caught sight of the group. His eyes widened, then did the thing that Louise wasn't ready for before. They glided down, then up her form. She could feel his eyes as they drifted around her body. She wasn't sure how to feel about the fire that kindled inside her at the sight of him looking at her. He then smiled a new smile; this smile made that fire turn into an inferno.

Harper started pushing Louise again, so she had to straighten up and walk normally. Normal, but with a slight sway to her hips, her back straight, and chest out. His new smile grew as they got closer, making him look like he found his treasure after a long expedition. Louise kept her cool. She ignored him while standing close to him and gestured to the bartender. When the bartender came up to her, she ordered her drink and looked around.

"Next round on me." As the rest of the group ordered, she felt Carlos' eyes still on her. She wasn't ready to look at him. She was still trying to put out the inferno that his look caused.

"Hello, Louise." Her knees nearly buckled. He came in close and whispered the greeting in her ear. His scent was mesmerizing, and she knew that whatever cologne he wore ruined it for any other man.

"Um, hi, Carlos." She still wouldn't look at him. She couldn't imagine how her face looked. She was emotionally out of control and was afraid of what she might do to him. Everyone else finished their drink orders.

"This round is on me. I would like a bourbon on the rocks." He handed his card to the bartender. Louise swallowed hard, trying to control herself. She looked over at her friends, but none of them offered her any help. They stood around pretending to talk to each other. Louise knew that she would have to address him. She would rather later than sooner, but the bartender would be awhile with their drink order.

Louise finally looked in his direction, her eyes immediately at his chest. And as slowly as he'd looked at her, she slowly made her way up. Again, she was happy for the height boost as her eyes finally met his. The warmth she was normally used to turned all the way up. She felt the fire in his eyes that matched the one inside her. She smiled at him, hoping that the smile looked simple and sweet.

"Thanks for the drink."

"You're welcome."

Louise looked forward again, not knowing how to disengage her awkwardness. She felt his movement to face the group.

"Can you all watch our drinks?" He put his hand out to her.

She hesitated a few seconds, then took it. He walked her to the dance floor.

The upbeat dance song that was playing transitioned into a slower song as they maneuvered around the other dancers on the floor. As far as Louise was concerned, the other people in the club disappeared the moment Carlos held her hand.

The song playing had an Afro-Caribbean beat. Carlos pulled Louise close. Louise lost all connection to her body. She was stiff as he tried to dance with her. When she tried to move, she stepped on his foot. She pulled away from him to walk away. Carlos touched her chin. She looked up at him. The familiar smile she loved and was back. He leaned in close.

"Relax." He said, and she smiled. He held out his hands for her to grab. He started leading her in a simple dance, and she relaxed. They found a rhythm as he pulled her closer. They were still holding each other's hands. He let go of one of her hands and placed his on her waist. Louise finally leaned in closer to him, the length of her melding with the length of him. The music changed back to a faster beat but the two of them still swayed, looking into each other eyes.

Eventually, they felt the people bumping into them. This woke Louise out of the dream she was in. She pulled away, but Carlos continued to dance, now to the rhythm of the song. She started to really relax and enjoy dancing to the fast dance beats.

After a few songs, she pulled him away from the dance floor. They found Jamal and Silas at a high-top table with their now watered-down drinks. Louise grabbed her glass and took a sip. Jamal and Silas both stared at her. Silas was excited and cheesing hard. Jamal smiled, but he was more guarded.

"Where are Harp and Ang?" Jamal pointed to the dance floor, but Louise couldn't see them through all the people. The table only had three seats, so Carlos motioned for her to sit. She climbed onto the bar stool and Carlos stood next to her, resting his arm around the back of her chair. He traced his fingers up and down her arm. The earlier inferno was still burning. She had no idea that it could get hotter.

"Are you two finished dancing?" Louise asked. Silas looked at Jamal.

"He is." Silas said. Jamal yawned to prove the point. Louise drunk the last of her drink and grasped Silas' hand.

"We have to make sure this night was worth it." She looked at Carlos. "Do you mind?" He shook his head and smiled her smile. She was mad at herself for feeling the need to ask his permission. She should be able to dance with her cousin-in-law any time she wanted to.

As Silas and Louise walked away, Louise looked back to see Jamal lean over to talk to Carlos. She might have done the wrong thing. She would have given anything to know what Jamal said.

Jamal lasted another hour before he and Silas headed out. Louise checked her phone. This was the latest she'd been out in years. Harper was nowhere to be found, as she had probably found some guy to make out with in a corner. Carlos, Angie, and her were sitting at a table drinking water. Louise was feeling tipsy and didn't want to deal with a hangover two weeks in a row.

Angie stood up to look for Harper, but Carlos stopped her and went himself. Angie looked over and smiled.

"He is way better than I expected. When are you going to lock that down?" Angie said.

"You sound like Harper. We have a professional relationship."

"If any of my coworkers looked at me the way he looks at you, I would be in trouble."

"It doesn't help that you and Harper made me wear this breast-exposing shirt. I have been scared all night I might flash someone." Angie laughed at her, then she scooted closer.

"Seriously, I don't know much about him. Is he worth it? He is cute for a fun fling, but we both know you don't do flings."

"He is so...," Louise waved her hands around. "I can't describe him. At first, he was this charming guy who everyone likes. I wanted to believe he was a little vapid. But then we had these talks, and he is so...not superficial, sometimes. And he is so smart. He found ways around some of our biggest issues. Someone that attractive shouldn't be this perfect."

"Oh no, sweetie."

"What?" Louise looked at Angie.

"Girl, you are gone." Angie laughed again. "I haven't seen you like this in a long time."

"I told Jamal that it's a crush. You know how I am." Angie's brows furrowed.

"What do you mean, I know how you are?"

"I blow things up to more than what they are. Like I said, I have a crush and he will be gone next week. So, it doesn't even matter."

"How do you think you are 'blowing this up'?"

Louise shrugged. "Tomorrow when all of this is gone," she gestured to her outfit and face, "I will be back to my normal self, and he will not look at me in any kind of way."

"Girl! Give yourself more credit than that. You know the power you have. Don't lose your confidence now. This is not the woman who walked up to a professional football player in Atlanta and had his nose open all night. You know what you bring to any table."

Louise smiled at her friend. "I guess."

"No 'I guess', babe. He would be lucky if you chose him. With that being said, I saw his looks. He likes you too. And it's more than your outfit tonight."

They looked up to see Harper and Carlos walking towards them. Harper was leaning a little too much on Carlos, signaling that she had had too much to drink. The group made it to the car, with Angie driving and Harper insisting on getting in the front. Carlos had taken a rideshare here, so needed to ride back with them. Louise squeezed herself as close to the passenger door as she could. She looked out the window to avoid the eyes that she felt. She stayed that way the entire car ride.

When they made it back to her house, Angie helped Harper to the door. Louise lingered at her car, looking after them. Carlos didn't move either.

"Will I see you at 6:30 a.m.?" He asked. Louise shook her head. Carlos releases a long breath. "Thank goodness. I have been struggling to keep up with your schedule. I feel like I have been in the bed at eight every night."

She started laughing. "You didn't have to. You could have slept in."

"No, I couldn't have. We never would have gotten to a place where you respected me if I didn't show the same work ethic as you."

"Not true!"

"True."

"Maybe. But I don't expect everyone to keep the same hours as me. I didn't expect you to."

"That's why I had to. It also allowed me to get to know you better." He smiled his coy smile. She meandered to her door.

"You don't have to worry about 6:30. My 5 a.m. alarm won't get much love in the morning." She stopped and turned fully to him. He reached and began caressing her cheek. She leaned into him.

"Kiss her already!" Harper yelled out the cracked door.

"Sorry!" Louise heard Angie call to them, and the door really closed. She looked back at Carlos and they both started laughing.

"What time should I expect to see you tomorrow?" He said, still laughing.

"Around 8. Maybe we can have breakfast in the dining room." He had the 100-watt smile she hadn't seen in a while. He took her waist and pulled her in for a hug.

"See you in the morning." He then kissed her on the cheek and ushered to her door.

CHAPTER 14

THE NEXT MORNING, Louise was hesitant about her breakfast date. She didn't even know if it could be called a date, and thought she asked him out. She had never asked anybody out before. What if it wasn't a date, but more of a business meeting? After the chaste kiss he gave her last night, she had no choice but to think that they were friends. Nothing wrong with being friends. But she didn't want to be his friend. She wouldn't be able to be his friend. Friends was all they could afford, though; he would leave next week. There wasn't a reason for him to stay. Unless she found a reason for him to stay.

When she made it to the estate, she looked immediately for his seat. He was there looking casual and delicious, with *that smile* on his face. He stood when she entered. She stopped a little way from him and smiled. He closed the distance in two steps and pulled her in for a hug. A few seconds later, she looked up into his eyes and he leaned into her. She remembered where they were and stepped back, looking over at the front desk agent. He turned away quickly, looking at the computer.

Carlos looked over and smiled, grabbing her hand, and kissing it. He walked her to the dining room, and they took a table.

"No private room this morning." She mused.

"You didn't give me enough time to plan," he said, laughing. "I woke up twenty minutes ago."

She looked at his hair, and the curls were damp. A solitary droplet of water trickled in front of his ear. She reached out and wiped it away. Carlos grasped her hand and didn't let go. *Do friends hold hands?* she asked herself.

A server came by to take their drink orders. The estate offered a buffet-style breakfast, so Louise and Carlos got up to fix their plates. Louise kept it simple and probably a little boring. When they made it back to the table, Carlos looked at her plate with his eyebrow raised. Louise shrugged and sat down.

"Be right back." Carlos said and went back to the buffet area. When he came back, he had an array of pastries. She smiled as he sat down.

"What's this?" she asked.

"The breakfast you chose is for work. We are supposed to be relaxing and resting."

"Oh, are we? I'm going to work after this."

"Oh, are you?" He had a sly smile.

"What are you up to?" He shrugged.

"I told you; I've only been up for a few minutes. That's no time to get much done. Much."

"Carlos…" He beamed.

"Say it again." She blushed and shook her head. Carlos captured her hand and repeated himself.

"Carlos." This time, she let his name curl over her tongue. She boldly looked him in his eyes. He put his other hand over his chest and sat back. The side of his mouth curled up, then he kissed her wrist of the hand he was holding. She caught her breath. The inferno raged again.

"I thought we can spend the day together." He said, then kissed her wrist again. It surprised her she wasn't on the floor.

"I have to work," she reminded him.

"Let me have the day. Please?" She was completely done. Her head nodded in agreement, but she was only aware of their fingers entwined and the burning on the spot he kissed. With her free hand, she grabbed her glass of water and drunk most of it down. She commandeered her other hand back to eat. Carlos was still eyeing her with his question unanswered. She started putting food in her mouth to give her time to calm her racing heart.

"Ok," she said while she finished chewing her food. "I need to check my email."

"I'll give you ten minutes to check your email, then you are mine." The underlying rumble as he said the last part almost took her out. She was reconsidering agreeing to his plan. She didn't know how she was going to spend the day with him, trying to manage her inferno and him adding coals to the fire.

Carlos was true to his word. After breakfast, he walked her to her office, then went to the lobby as she checked her email. Ten minutes later, he was at her door waiting for her to finish. Her eyes fixated on his relaxed posture leaning on her door frame. She could get used to this. She could get used to Carlos Hernández pulling her from work every evening and them walking hand in hand back to her house.

She shook the thought out of her head. He would be gone next week. She grew sad, and her face reflected it because Carlos rushed to her desk. He knelt beside her.

"Are you alright? Was there bad news?"

"No. Sorry, I just…"

"Don't apologize. What can I do?" Louise shook her head. She didn't know what to say. She wanted to know why they were doing this. Why did he want to spend the day with her and then leave? She looked at him. He looked genuinely concerned for her. She gave him a small smile. Can she be honest with him?

"I'm ok, really." She brightened. "What did you plan in these ten minutes?"

He smiled, but still looked worried.

"I thought you can give me a tour of the town. Jamal and Silas were great tour guides, but I want to know the town from your point of view. And there is a festival going on today."

"Oh yeah, it is time for the Sugar Plum Festival. But they do something every weekend in town. I hope you have warm clothing. There will be a lot of snow activities."

"Good! I'll put on more layers. Promise me you will have your most Christmassy outfit on." She laughed at him.

"I will try."

An hour later, Louise was in her car with Carlos and Angie. Angie would visit her parents for the day while Carlos and Louise went on their date. Louise kept inviting Angie to some events, but Angie said no. Angie was determined to leave the two alone. They dropped Angie at her parents' house. She told Louise not to worry about her. She would catch a ride from Harper and use her spare key.

"I will have my noise cancelling headphones on while I work. Bye!" she yelled as she closed the door and hurried up the walk. Carlos was grinning. Louise was not.

Parking at the town's square was packed, so she parked at her parent's house, and they walked over. Louise stopped to see if her parents were home. The house was empty, so she guessed they were already at the festival.

"Did you grow up in this house?"

"Yes. My mom keeps my bedroom the same. It's looks like it did when I left for college."

"Oh, I have to see that." He started walking back to the house. Louise grabbed his arm and pulled him towards the town. He used that opportunity to put his arm around her. They walked this way the few blocks to the square. The closer they got to people, though, Louise got nervous and left from under his arm.

"What's wrong?" He touched her arm and pulled her back to him. He stared at her, but she couldn't look him in the eyes.

"What are we doing?" She finally looked at him.

"I thought we were enjoying this beautiful day."

"You know what I mean. Your arm is around me. The flirting. What is this?"

He stepped closer to her.

"I enjoy being around you, Louise. I wanted to be with you, away from our jobs. I want to get to know *you*."

Louise wanted to mention the elephant in the room. He would be gone in a few days, and she would be heartbroken. She couldn't do it because she was enjoying being around him so much. She took a deep breath.

"Ok. But I'm sure that we are the topic of a few rumor mills as it is. Small town and all. Let's keep it friendly." She held out her hand. He grasped it and they shook. His mouth turned up in the corners in his slyest smile. She saw the twinkle in his eye, letting her know he was going to be naughty all day. She let go and dashed away.

He was good for a couple of hours as they joined the festivities. The town's annual Sugar Plum festival mixed arts and crafts booths and snow activities. They spent the first part of the tour looking at all the arts and crafts booths. Louise couldn't help but to buy something at almost every booth. Carlos, the gentleman he was, carried the accumulating bags.

Harper had a booth, and they stopped there. Harper and Louise chatted while Carlos browsed through Harper's art. They walked to the next booth that sold Louise's favorite jams.

"Harper is an amazing artist." Carlos said while Louise tasted one of the new jams. She nodded at his statement.

"No offense, but why is she still here?" Louise pointed to all the jams she wanted to buy for the vendor to wrap up. She finally turned back to Carlos.

"Try this." She put a piece of bread with the jam in his mouth, ignoring the smile as he chewed. "No offense taken. We think Harper should be in galleries in the biggest cities. I'm sure I'm biased, but she is the best artist I've ever seen."

"Then why won't she go to New York or L.A.? I know a couple of gallery owners I could introduce her to."

"Unfortunately, she doesn't believe in her work like we do. People always are buying her art in the estate." Carlos's eyebrows raised.

"That's her art at the estate," she continued. "You are in...526. She created that landscape while in high school."

"You remembered my room number?"

"What?" The change in subject confused her.

"Since you remember my room number, why don't you come by?" He stepped in close to her. Despite the surrounding cold, her inferno reignited.

"Friendly." She said.

"I'm being friendly by inviting you to my room." Carlos smiled that dangerous smile. She hadn't forgotten that he cheated her out of a taste of his mouth twice now. She heard her name being called. She jerked around to one of her old friends waving. She was relieved, but mad. Despite knowing it wouldn't be good for her, she wanted to explore that moment with Carlos.

After buying up the whole festival, they went to play some games. Carlos was like a kid. He said he hadn't been able to play in the snow since his family moved from New York. Louise had a ball watching him throw snowballs with the children. Then Carlos dragged her to the snowman building contest.

They put together an ugly snowman that looked like he was on the verge of falling over. Their snowman might have been straighter if Carlos hadn't continuously distracted Louise. He kept 'helping' her by putting his arms around her to guide her hands over the snow. He also used their closeness to whisper instructions in her ear, causing the inferno to burn hotter. She kept trying to escape his embrace, but he would capture her again.

They left the snowman contest, in last place, to go to the hot cocoa truck. While on the way to the truck, Louise and Carlos ran into Jamal and Silas.

"Well, don't you two look cute." Silas said.

"Si." Jamal said, a warning in his tone. Louise could see the curiosity in Jamal's eyes. Last night when he'd left the club, they were together and now they were still together. Louise gave Jamal a small shake of her head. He looked relieved.

"We are heading to get some hot cocoa." Louise said.

"We will join you." Jamal said.

Carlos and Silas fell into a conversation while Jamal started walking slowly. Louise slowed her pace to match his.

"So?" she asked him. Jamal was looking at Carlos's back.

"Anything happen?"

"No. If by anything you mean he stayed at my house, or I stayed in his room. We have been friendly."

"Have you?" Jamal looked at her. She nodded. They made it to the truck. Carlos and Silas were in line getting their drinks. Louise and Jamal stopped, still out of earshot of the other two.

"Jay, don't be worried."

"Harper wants this to happen. That is why she invited him out last night. But she has a habit of not considering the consequences." Louise looked at him. "We all love you and want you to be happy. I like Carlos. If he was based near us, I would tell you to go for it."

"I know Jay. I know that I have an expiration date with him. And I'm already sad about his leaving."

"I talked to him last night."

"I know. Were you nice?"

Jamal faked a shock face. "I'm always nice." They both laughed. They looked over at Carlos and Silas, who were a couple of people from the window.

"Well?" she asked.

"I told him not to hurt you. I also said that if he was playing a game or wanted a conquest that he should find someone else. There are a few ladies on the staff that would happily grant him that. I told him to keep pursuing you only if he was serious. Or I would make sure they never find him."

"You didn't say the last part, did you?" Jamal nodded.

"You are my favorite cousin and best friend. I would do anything for you."

"So that's why he didn't kiss me last night."

"You tried?" Louise shrugged. The men were walking back to them.

"You think he is serious?" But the men made it back to them before Jamal could answer.

"'Thank you, baby." Jamal said to Silas as they kissed.

"Now, who are the cute ones?" Louise said, winking at Silas.

"We will always out-cute any couple. I would say what couple are trying to take our trophy, but I don't want to get in trouble." Silas said. Louise sipped her hot cocoa, looking away from Silas and Carlos.

"So, what are you two getting into?" Silas asked.

"Hopefully, some food soon." Carlos said.

"No one told you to waste all your energy having a snowball fight with those kids." She laughed, and he naturally put his arm around her.

"I couldn't help myself. I haven't been around snow since I was a kid." He directed the last part to Jamal and Silas, who were both looking at his arm. She twisted out of his embrace and started walking to a nearby restaurant.

"This is my favorite place to eat in town." She waved Carlos to follow. "You two can come."

CHAPTER 15

L OUISE AND CARLOS had a great lunch with Jamal and Silas. Then the group broke up for Carlos to play powder-puff football with a bunch of guys at the park. Louise was never much for sports, but it was fun to watch Carlos from the sidelines. It gave Louise time to study his form without him seeing.

When they finally made it back to the estate, it was later that evening. Louise was nervous. She didn't know where the night would go from here. She was tempted to invite him to her house for dinner, but she wasn't ready for the pressure associated with him being in her home. Neither one of them made a move when she parked her car. She snuck a look at him, and his face was emotionless. She went to open her door.

"I had a great time today." Louise said. She opened her car door. He seemed to shake himself and smiled at her. It was her smile, genuine and sweet.

"Thank you for taking the day off for me." He held her hand. She stared at their hands.

"Thank you for inviting me." They held hands for a while. She let go of the door and it closed back. The overhead light eventually went out. She gazed into his eyes then, the shadows giving her courage. He leaned to her, only stopping when their foreheads met. All she had to do was bring her chin up a little.

Her neck wouldn't move. Her fear, the one that fought his flirtations all day, wouldn't let her move to bring them closer. She knew that if she kissed him, if she did more with him, she would cross a line she can't come back from. Right now, in this moment, she convinced herself that she could still let him go. She breathed in and brought her head back, letting go of his hand. They both got out of the car.

"Same time tomorrow?" he asked.

"You will be sore tomorrow, so sleep in," she said, smiling at him.

"Louise, I'm still in my prime. I won't be sore. That is, after I soak in some Epson salt." She had to hold on to the car from the vision of him soaking in a tub.

"Are you ok?" He came to her and held her wrist.

"I'm tired. After walking up and down the town a million times." She hoped her smile distracted him from her flushed face.

He walked her to the front door. "I'll see you in the morning, then."

"It will be later, like 8 again. And tomorrow I need to get some work done. So, no distractions from you." She pointed at him. He held her finger and kissed it.

"No promises." He said. Then he was walking back to the estate.

THE NEXT MORNING, Louise was back in her routine. At the door of Cummings estate, she stopped to look at the ceiling carvings before looking for Carlos. She smiled widely at him.

"Did you sleep well?" She asked. He nodded.

"Are you sore?" she asked, her eyebrow raised.

"Only a little." He waved her over. She grabbed his hands and attempted to pull him up, but he pulled her down on his lap. He surrounded her with his arms. She stopped breathing. They were nose to nose.

"Good morning." He said. She felt his lips move so close to hers.

"Get a room!" she heard Angie yell. Louise jumped up and barked an awkward laugh. She saw Angie heading to the dining room. Louise walked; half ran to her office.

Carlos entered her office a minute after with his work bag. He was relaxed, on the edge of a laugh. He sat and pulled out his laptop. He worked without saying a word. She wanted to say something, but she knew he would start laughing and she wouldn't get anything done. They worked silently for a few hours.

At lunch, Louise was done for the day. The day before, he promised her mother's friend that she would make her famous shortbread cookies. She felt like today would be a good baking day. She was sitting back in her chair, staring off into space. Carlos stood and stretched.

"You want to grab lunch?" She nodded at his question. "Good. I have some reports I have been putting off and they are due tomorrow. You are a distraction, Louise Cummings."

Louise jumped up, pointing at Carlos, ready to defend herself.

"A beautiful distraction," he said, and all her steam disappeared. He took her hand and guided her around the desk. When they settled in for lunch, he asked if he could order for them.

"Sure. Let's see how well you know me." She said.

"I know you. That's why I'm not ordering a dry turkey sandwich. I don't understand why it must be so dry." He bunched his face up, and she laughed.

"I don't like mayo. It's white and yucky. Mustard is too strong for anything but a hot dog. There aren't too many other spreads I can put on a sandwich."

"How about Miracle Whip?"

"That is the same as mayo and I don't care what anybody says!" They both laughed.

"Ok, but you at least can get it grilled or something. The cheese could play as a spread."

"I never thought of that. Maybe I'll try it tomorrow." The server came, and Carlos ordered them the soup of the day and a salad without goat cheese.

"Yesterday there was a lot going on, so I didn't get to ask you the questions I have." Carlos said.

"You have questions?"

"Yes, I have a lot of them. There is so much I want to know about you." Carlos smiled. "Starting with the most obvious one. Why did you drop the 'Mr. Hernández'?"

Louise's tongue stuck to the roof of her mouth. Carlos had a big grin on his face.

"Never mind, we will get back to that one. Seriously though, I want to know why you stop and look at the ceiling every morning? That one has been driving me crazy."

She relaxed. She could answer this question.

"That answer comes with a story. My great-great-grandfather made the carving in the ceiling. He was a former slave that came from Louisiana after they freed the slaves. He somehow made his way to this town where the estate stood. It was owned by the Murphy family, and he worked as one of the farm hands. He was great at woodworking, so the family hired him to carve the wooden columns. He continued working for the family, meeting his wife, who was their housekeeper, and they raised their family. There was a fire that unfortunately killed the original owner and his son. The wife didn't want to keep the estate, so she left to live with her remaining family. My two-times great grandfather kept up the estate with his family and made extra money with his woodworking. They eventually got permission from the owner to run a lodging business out of the estate.

"When he died, my great grandfather took over as caretaker of the lodge. He bought the place from the original owners and renovated it to have more rooms. When I stop to look up at the carvings, it reminds me of my history. It reminds me of the sacrifices that were made so that I could be here to run the estate. I'm grateful to them. So, I stand to give myself the strength I need and to show them gratitude."

Carlos was silent. He stared at her in what she could only guess as amazement.

"That is a wonderful story. I could tell the carvings were original, but the story behind them is even more amazing. I see why you are so proud of the Cummings."

"Thank you. I'm so grateful that my family trusted me enough to run it. That is what made me so passionate and stubborn."

"I understand. This is your legacy, not just an estate."

"Yes." The server came with their food. They ate in silence for a while. Louise cleared her throat before continuing.

"Can I ask you a question?"

"Sure." He said while wiping his mouth.

"It's kind of a sensitive question. Last time we broached it, you shut down a little." He nodded his head for her to continue. "Why do you hate your job so much? You are amazing at it."

"I don't hate my job. It's a good job to have."

"You don't hate it, but at the tree lighting, you shut down when I questioned you about it."

"You are right. I'm sorry about that. I do like what I do, for the most part. It's aspects of the job that I hate."

"Like giving reports and having paying clients yell at you." She smiled at him.

"In your defense, *you* didn't pay for our consultation. But that part is not fun sometimes. I have had clients that blamed me personally for the issues I have discovered. I have found illegal things in the past that I have had to call the FCC or other agencies about. Those situations weren't great."

"Wow. That would suck. Is that it?"

"No, that part isn't so bad. Most of my clients are eventually grateful. Especially when we collaborate on a plan to correct the issues. I like the collaboration and working to help smaller businesses do what's needed to help them grow."

"You sound excited now. Why did you shut down before?"

"I enjoy working with our clients. I don't like the direction my company is taking. Shoot, I shouldn't say that to a client."

"And why you also shut down before? It's difficult complaining about your company to someone who hired them. Even if it wasn't directly. I understand a little better now."

"I didn't really notice that I shut down. Again, I'm sorry." He paused for a second. "What made you think I shut down?"

Louise looked away. She wasn't sure if she should tell him how much time she spent reading every detail of his face.

"You have a smile that you use to 'charm' people or whatever. But whenever that smile comes, I know that it's not the real you. It's like a mask."

He nodded, not looking at her. He focused on a spot on the table. The server came to collect their dishes. She continued to look at him, waiting for a response. He finally looked at her. Carlos then reached over for her hand. She placed her hand in his.

"I spent years cultivating this persona at work to make people comfortable around me. People make all kinds of assumptions about me in my position. It can be easy to use charm and the assumption that people have about my intelligence to get things done."

"It can be hard trying to fight through other people's prejudices."

"I'm sure you can understand."

"A Black-owned luxury estate?" She scoffed. "No, I know nothing about that." They both smiled. "You should see the looks we get when a customer asks for a manager and Jamal, or I step from the back room."

"At the beginning of my career with Willis and Spencer, when I started consulting, I had a manager suggest I change my last name. To something less ethnically noticeable." Louise sure her face showed the shock that she felt. Carlos shrugged his shoulders.

"I would never change my name for a job, but I had to fight for clients. That same manager would say that the clients were unsure of me because of how new I was to the position and things like that. Come to find out that he wouldn't put me up for projects. He ended up being the problem."

"So, what happened?"

"He got fired for sexual harassment. Men like that have all kinds of issues. When he left, my new manager gave me a chance. I became the best, if I say so myself, consultant they have."

"I'm sorry you had to go through all of that."

"Thank you. But that is the reason for the smile, or mask, as you called it." Carlos smiled her smile and held her other hand. "The only other person who regularly calls me out on it is my mom. I have been trying to use that smile on her my whole life."

Louise smiled. She like learning this tidbit about his family. She put it in the Carlos' family file in her brain with all the other little tidbits she'd pick up. This Carlos file was growing, but with a destination to the trash.

CHAPTER 16

W HEN THEY MADE it back to her office, Carlos settled back in to do some work. Louise was ready to go, but she also wanted to watch his eyes as they scanned his computer. She stared at him for a bit. She could see her smile playing at the edges of his mouth.

"I told you. 'A distraction'". Carlos finally looked at her, his full smile on display. "I'm trying to work."

"You know how I have felt then." She smiled back at him. He shook his head and looked back at the computer screen. Louise still stared. Only looking up when Jamal came to the door.

"Hey, Jay. What are you doing here on a Sunday?"

"Hey you two. Silas went to visit his parents today. He had to be up early; they are baptizing his niece today. I couldn't go back to sleep, so I came in. I had to catch up on the millions of emails you sent."

"Two emails."

"I'm about done, though. How you work all day on the weekends, I'll never know."

"I'm about to leave anyway, so there." Carlos looked up at her.

"It's only 1 p.m. I know you can't be leaving yet." Jamal said.

"Today is a baking day. Mrs. Taylor asked for the shortbread cookies. I may as well make enough for the season."

Jamal moaned. "We need at least 2 dozen." Carlos looked at Jamal. "Louise makes the best shortbread cookies. She got the recipe from our grandmother. But she perfected it by putting these jams on them and other stuff. Wait until you try them."

Carlos's eyebrows raised when he looked back at Louise. She shrugged.

"You haven't had any of her cooking yet, have you Carlos?" Jamal asked. Louise pointedly looked at Jamal with a frown.

"I haven't."

"Oh, you are missing out. Louise, you ought to cook for Carlos tonight. Make a traditional Sunday dinner like we used to do." Louise wanted to throw something at Jamal, but he smiled. Carlos was also still looking at her.

"Ok...I guess I can throw something together." She stammered.

"Good. And Carlos let me know how it was tomorrow." Jamal waved and walked off. His smirk let Louse know he was aware of the bomb he let off in her office. For someone so worried about her heart, why was he playing games?

"What time do you want me to come by?"

"Let's say 6. It will give me some time to shop and bake some. So um, see you then." She got up and gather her stuff and walked to the door. "You can stay here to work." She hurried off.

At 6 p.m. on the dot, her doorbell rang. She looked at her phone to see Carlos standing at the door with flowers that had to come from the gift shop. She smiled before yelling for Angie to let him in. Angie tried her best to get away when she found out Carlos was coming over. Louise insisted she needed support. Determined to not fall for Carlos, she admitted she was crushing over him. She could get over a crush.

He came into her kitchen. "If I had transportation, I could've gotten you better flowers than these."

"These are nice." She wiped her hands and took them from him. She got a vase out of her cabinet and put water and the flowers in it. She then led him to the dining room. "The food will be ready in a sec. Here, can you open this wine for us? Angie will join us. She is staying with me until Christmas eve."

"I thought you said she had family here."

"She does. She came in early for me."

"And with my family, a little time can go a long way." Angie said, walking into the room. "Hey Carlos." Angie extended her hand. They shook.

"I have to warn you, Ang is not as sweet as Harper." Louise said, going back to the kitchen.

"I didn't rightfully get to interrogate you at the club either." Angie said. Louise saw the cringe Carlos had as she walked out the door.

Angie took it easy on Carlos during dinner. She only slung him low-ball questions. Louise enjoyed the night because it allowed her to get to know Carlos a little better without the pressure of leading the conversation. She spent a lot of time watching the back and forth between the two.

Carlos offered to do the dishes after they finished eating. He gathered the dishes and took them to the kitchen.

"I like him." Angie whispered. She stood up. "I know you are scared. Give him a chance. But don't sleep with him." She winked and went off to her room.

Louise smiled and gathered the last of the dishes to take to the kitchen. Carlos was eyeing the cookies cooling on the counter.

"So, these are the famous cookies?" She nodded. He walked close to the cookie laden counter.

"I promised those to someone. Back up, Mr. Hernández."

She warned. He smiled at her and grabbed a cookie and put it into his mouth before she could reach him. He closed his eyes and moaned. She was used to this reaction to the cookies. She enjoyed his reaction more than she ever had before.

"Jamal didn't lie. These are outstanding."

"Thanks." She pulled him away from the counter. "Like I said, I promised those to someone. Now you will have to help me make the replacement. I'll also make you some, I guess."

After putting the dishes in the dishwasher, Carlos helped Louise make the next batch of cookies. She mixed the ingredients and put the formed dough in a bowl.

"These will go into the fridge to rest." She pulled a couple of bowls out. "These are ready to be cut and baked." She took out one dough ball and put it on the counter with a little flour. She went to her pantry to grab him an apron. She put it around his waist and tied it behind him.

"Now roll these out and use this cutter."

"You are very bossy!" She nodded and headed to the other dough ball and rolled them out. Carlos stood there gingerly rolling the ball.

"Have you never baked before?" She asked.

"No. My mom had two boys. She spent much of our childhood running us out of the kitchen. And don't look at me like that. I can cook, some." Louise shook her head and laughed. She put her rolling pin down and got close to Carlos. She put her hands around his on the rolling pin he had.

"First, you want to make sure you are starting from the center. You need pressure like this." She pushed down on his hands. "Then you roll back and forth until you form a circle."

After they did a few rolls, she let go of him. She brushed a hair from her head with the back of her hand. Carlos looked at her and laughed.

"What?"

"You have flour all over your face." She shook her head and reached across him for a dish towel. He placed his hand on her waist. She looked up at him. He had a fire in his eyes that reminded her that her fire had never gone out. He bent over and finally put his lips to hers. It was the softest of kisses. He pulled back. Louise abandoned the towel and grabbed his shirt, pulling him towards her. She saw the smirk before she enveloped his mouth again. This kiss was full of the fire and passion she had been waiting for. And it was well worth the wait.

Louise let go of Carlos' shirt and ran her fingers through his hair. She had wanted to do that since day one. He began kissing her neck and groaned into her as she played with his curls. He pushed her against the counter.

"We can't hurt the cookies." She frowned a little, not because of the cookies, but because she's foolishly broken their kiss. Carlos laughed, walking back to her opposite counter. Louise didn't know what to do now. She felt awkward. She turned to the dough and started cutting out the shapes. Carlos came behind her to put one arm around her waist and the other one in her hand. He helped her cut the cookies.

When they were done, she put the cut cookies on a tray and into the pre-heated oven.

"I think I enjoy making cookies." He said. She went to push him, but he kissed her again. This one with a little less heat.

"This is you distracting me for the record." She turned and finished the dough she was working on.

They made a few more dozen cookies. She then took him to her couch so they could watch a movie. She picked some movie that was number one on the streaming service. It didn't take long; she fell asleep while he was holding her.

She didn't know how long he let her sleep. He eventually shook her awake.

"I better get back to my room." She nodded, and they stood up.

"I'm sorry I went to sleep."

"This is how you can be at work at 6:30 a.m. bright and beautiful." She reached up and kissed him.

"The saying is bright and early."

"I know what I said." They kissed again before he finally straightened up and walked to the door. "You keep giving me reason to get excited about 6:30 a.m., Ms. Cummings."

CHAPTER 17

THE BUTTERFLIES IN Louise's stomach felt like eagles as she headed to the estate the next day. She woke up wondering if the previous night was a dream. She also woke up to a barrage of text messages. She realized she made a mistake texting the group with Harper, Angie, and Jamal about the kiss. Harper worked the overnight shift, so was wide awake when her text came in. Harper had nothing but time to contemplate through the text of the ramifications of Louise's and Carlos' romance. Angie and Jamal were up to respond to her texts, and they got very detailed and inappropriate. Louise was glad that her phone was off the previous night. She spent too much time reading through the texts, almost missing her 6:30 a.m. arrival to work.

Even though she didn't want to be late to work, she still stood outside the doors of the estate. After a few minutes, and with her teeth chattering, she saw Carlos walking towards her. He had his hands in his pockets as he was without his coat.

"Are you going to stand there all day? He asked.

"Maybe." She stammered through her chattering teeth.

"Louise." Carlos reached out to her. She was too cold to be

her usual stubborn self. Louise took Carlos's hand, and they walked through the door.

"What was that about?" he asked. Harper started whooping behind the front desk.

"That." She responded. She walked to her office. Carlos was right behind her. When they settled, he looked at her questionably.

"I made the mistake of mentioning our night to my soon to be ex-friends." She paused and looked at her hands. "I also was nervous. I was scared we changed something. What if you felt differently or regretted..."

Louise heard Carlos get up. She looked up as he walked around her desk. He pulled her from her chair and kissed her deeply. She pulled away from him after a few minutes. She looked into his eyes.

"I do not regret last night or any second I spend with you. I regret I waited so long to do this." He said and kissed her on the nose, then rested his head on hers. Louise hated to break from their embrace, but they were at work. She pushed him away and pointed to his chair.

"That is the only time we can do that while on duty. While we are working, you are Mr. Hernández and I'm Ms. Cummings." She straightened her suit jacket and sat down.

"Ok Ms. Cummings." Carlos said, but Louise saw a twinkle in his eye that she knew to be trouble.

Carlos stayed tame most of the morning. Louise suspected it was because of the reports that he had due. She turned into their report to the board, so she was waiting for feedback from them. There wasn't anything else that Carlos needed to do within the estate.

That afternoon, though, Carlos must have been done with his work because he was determined to keep Louise from hers. As Louise made her rounds at the estate, Carlos was on her heels.

Every moment he could, he would pull her to private corners and empty rooms so they could make out. It took them twenty minutes to get to the ballroom. A walk that took less than five minutes on her normal day.

She enjoyed every second, but her week was busy. The Estate's annual Christmas Eve dinner was at the end of the week. This party would follow the theme that they decorated the estate in, but it was exclusive to the adult members of the estate and town. It was a sit-down dinner with a dance afterwards. Louise had an event planner for the dinner, but they worked closely together to execute Louise's vision. Carlos was a major distraction.

By mid-week, after days of sneaking off to private areas of the estate and nights in her house learning about each other, Jamal called an intervention. He forced invited her to his house for dinner that night. Jamal was smart and sent his request through Carlos. Carlos didn't want to upset Jamal after the conversation that they had. There was no choice but to agree.

There was a hint of anger as she made her way to Jamal's and Silas's place. She felt robbed of spending the night with them instead of Carlos. He would be gone soon, and she wanted to soak up every second she could.

"Hey Si." Louise said and hugged Silas. She rolled her eyes at Jamal and walked past him.

"I didn't know you invited the ice queen." Silas said.

"She won't be mad long. Especially when she finds out you made lasagna." Jamal said. Louise perked up and walked to the kitchen.

"Jay must've known I would be mad if he convinced you to make lasagna." Louise said over her shoulder.

Silas met her in the kitchen. "Don't be too mad at him, Lou. We both wanted to see you."

Louise looked at Silas. Silas shrugged, then spoke again.

"Apparently, you went off the deep end. And looking at the light in your eyes, I can see why he is worried. I thought you were taking it slow?"

"I am...we are. We haven't slept together."

"That's not the slow I'm talking about." Silas said.

"Don't say anything, Si. She's not going to listen." Jamal yelled from the other room.

Silas shook his head and handed Louise a bottle of wine and bread to take in the dining room. Jamal and Silas had a cute ranch-style house that was very modern. It looked like it belonged to a social media influencer with all the white and cream. They even had a white Christmas tree with only silver decorations. The dining room table was glass with acrylic chairs. Louise felt like the house was too picture-perfect for her, but Jamal's and Silas's warmth made it a home.

They ate silently for a while as Louise lavished in Silas's amazing meal. She couldn't miss the looks that Jamal and Silas shared. She wiped her mouth and reached for a second helping.

"Ok Jay, give it to me." She said before taking another bite.

"Lou, do you know what you are doing?" Jamal asked.

"No, why don't you tell me?"

"I'm asking a serious question."

Louise sat back and finished chewing. She didn't know what she was doing. She was operating on instinct. She let her heart lead her with Carlos.

"Yes, I am enjoying the company of an amazing man. I'm living my best life. Sort of like how you and everyone else have been telling me what to do for the past ten years." She widened her eyes to Jamal.

"Lou, you have known Carlos for three weeks. You have been acting like a teenager for three days. Have you thought about when he leaves?"

"No."

"When is he leaving?"

"I don't know. When we get word back from the board."

"We may not get word back from them until after the holidays. Have you all talked about it?"

"No…"

"When are you going to talk about it?"

"Jay, baby, I thought we said this won't be an interrogation." Louise was glad Silas had interrupted Jamal. Jamal sat back in his chair and let out a breath.

"Jay, I'm happy. Isn't that worth it for now?" Louise asked.

Jamal looked at her. "Of course, your happiness matters. I care about what happens in a week. You are falling in love with that guy, and what has he offered you?"

"I'm not…" Louise looked over at Silas for help.

"Lou, you looked like a girl in love when you walked in." Silas said. Louise shook her head. She couldn't, she wouldn't fall in love. She hadn't even thought of that word.

"I'm not in love." She looked at them. "I am infatuated. I like him, but I'm not in love. I would know if I was in love. This isn't it."

They both looked doubtful. "Ok, I see you don't agree. What do you think I should do, then?"

"I think you should enjoy this." Silas said. Both Louise and Jamal looked at him, Jamal not smiling. "Lou, you have been so focused on making a success of Cummings that you let the other parts of your life fall by the wayside. Enjoy being with Carlos. It may be the real thing. And before you start, Jay, I fell in love with you the first moment I saw you. You took longer to fall for me, exactly one day longer. So don't stop her from figuring it out."

Louise smiled. She loved Silas. Having Jamal as her close

cousin and friend, she had seen him give away his heart to every low life he met. She was glad that he found someone who deserves his love. Jamal took Silas's hand. They shared a moment that had Louise focusing on her empty plate.

"I don't want you to get hurt, Lou. I know how that played out." Jamal's stare pierced through Louise. He was right; the last time she got her heart broken, she almost quit school. She was in her master's program and her off-and-on-again boyfriend was permanently off. Unfortunately, he also was 'on' with her close school friend. Louise was more than hurt—she felt embarrassed. She didn't feel like continuing in the program with that 'friend'.

"Jay, I hear you. This is going to hurt, isn't it?" She tried to laugh, but it came out dry. Jamal got up and hugged her. Then Silas hugged her from the other side.

"Ok! Let's kill the mush. Si, what have you made for dessert?" Louise asked.

"I didn't make desert. I was waiting for my cookies. Where are they?" Silas said. Louise rolled her eyes but went to get their package from her bag.

As she was leaving, Jamal walked her out.

"Ok, last-minute advice. What should I do?"

"I can't tell you what to do, honey. You know my stance. We all trust you. So, you must trust yourself. And it wouldn't hurt for you to talk about what happens when he leaves."

"Thanks."

LOUISE THOUGHT ABOUT Jamal's words the next day. She knew he was right, but she wasn't ready to pop the bubble she has been living in since Carlos kissed her. Her thoughts of their impending break needed to be at the forefront of her mind.

Carlos made that very hard as he decided that morning to put his chair next to hers.

"What are you doing?" she asked when he sat next to her.

"I'm tired of only having a piece of desk space. I need to spread out. You have too much room over here, anyway." He started pushing her files over to set up his laptop.

"Carlos..." she tried to sound stern but the smile she wore ruined her attempt. He leaned over to her, his nose touching hers. She closed her eyes to inhale his scent.

"You want me to move? I will, say the word." Carlos had to know that Louise wouldn't tell him to move. She swiveled her chair towards him and put her arms around his shoulders.

"You don't have to move, but you have to work." She pushed back from him and turned to her computer. She heard him snickering, but she also heard him opening his computer. They worked that way for the rest of the day.

"I want to have a nice dinner with you." Carlos said as they were leaving her office.

"I planned to cook us a wonderful dinner." she said.

"I know. But I don't want you have to be in your kitchen. I would cook for you, but I want you to keep liking me. And the dining room is a little too open." Carlos was right. Louise did still feel stiff on the estate. She didn't want to feed the gossip about the two of them.

"Do you like Italian?" Carlos nodded. "Good. It's a nice restaurant in town. We can go there."

"That is a plan. I can take you on a proper date."

"What, haven't you like our dates so far?" she asked. Carlos pulled her close. He leaned in and brought his mouth to hers.

"I love spending time with you, however you will allow me." Then he kissed her. Louise completely forgot where or when she was. They heard someone clear their throat. She moved back from Carlos's embrace. It was Jamal. He had a tight smile on his face.

"Hi Jamal." Carlos said, "I haven't seen a lot of you lately."

"Well, you both have been busy." Jamal responded, looking pointedly at Louise.

"Ok, I'm going to get dressed. Meet at my house in forty-five?" She started walking down the hall. Carlos had a new expression on his face. Louise felt the tension still emanating from Jamal.

"I'll walk you out, Jay." She grasped Jamal's arm, and they walked to the door. She said goodnight to Jamal. He said nothing more to Louise, and she was relieved. She would talk to Carlos tonight but didn't need anyone's voice in her head if she could help it.

Carlos was at her door thirty minutes later. She wasn't ready yet, so Angie let him in. When she made her way down the steps, his smile warmed her. He had on a simple blue suit. Louise was sure it was the suit he wore on the first day they met. She felt the same drop in her stomach as that day. She had on a brown sweater dress that hugged her curves. She put on a pair of tan stiletto boots so that Carlos wouldn't have to bend too far to kiss her. His eyes glowed, looking at her. Her heart started beating faster as he looked over at her.

"It's not your usual elf-wear."

"Are you disappointed?" Carlos came in close and put his hand on her waist. He shook his head before putting a peck on her lips. She heard Angie sigh. Louise looked over and Angie turned to face them with her chin in her hands.

"You two are so cute." Angie said.

"Bye!" Louise said, then took Carlos's hand.

Carlos offered to drive, wanting the date to feel 'official'. Louise directed him to the restaurant. She loved the fact that he was good at taking directions. She dealt with men before that would be stubborn about directions. Carlos wasn't overly macho, and Louise appreciated that. He was a gentleman in every form of the word.

"What do you like here?" Carlos asked.

"Everything," Louise laughed. "I'm serious. Everything is excellent here. The chef hand makes all the pasta. I wanted him to work for the estate, but he didn't think he could pull double duty with the restaurant. At the end, I won because I love Chef Henri. I get to come here anytime I crave pasta."

"What should I get then?"

"Mmmm, let me think. I can order you something that's not on the menu." Carlos smiled at her words. "A dry turkey sandwich."

Carlos burst out laughing. Louise joined into his laugh.

"Ok, how about some pasta?"

"That sounds way better than your turkey sandwich."

When the server came, Carlos let Louise order their meal. They also ordered a bottle of wine. Louise took a sip of the wine for a touch of courage. She didn't know if she should wait for this heavy conversation or to get it out. She wanted to continue to enjoy spending time with Carlos. When he leaned over and kissed her cheek, then grasped her hand, she let it wait.

"Finish the story about your worse Christmas." Carlos said.

"You remember that?" He nodded at her question. A couple of nights ago, they were talking about Christmas traditions. She slipped up and told him about her most miserable Christmas. She hated the story and rarely spoke about it.

"You don't want to hear about that." she said. Carlos squeezed the hand he was holding.

"I want to know everything about you." The warmth in his eyes opened her heart. She wanted him to know everything about her.

"Ok. It's a boring story. It's not super tragic or anything. My worse Christmas was the first year into my master's program. I convince myself that I wanted to graduate early, so I ended up taking a full workload. I also was working part time at a hotel as an assistant manager. I got overwhelmed with work and classes and ended behind. I couldn't go home that holiday. It was the first time I ever spent Christmas alone. Angie and Harper wanted to come spend it with me, but I couldn't take them away from their families. Then my parents were going to come. You've seen the work that goes into Christmas at Cummings, so I didn't feel right pulling them away.

"My friend also stayed. So, we had a small celebration together. I cooked, and we ate and watched movies. We watched all the depressing, make-you-want-to-cry holiday movies. It has become a tradition where I spend at least one day looking at the sad holiday movies. See, not so bad. It is the worst one for me."

Carlos stared at her. He kissed her hand. "Knowing how much your family and friends mean to you, I know that was a very sad Christmas for you. But what happened to the "friend"? You had a grimace when you mentioned them."

She felt herself grimace again. "That friend is a sore spot. I started dating a guy my sophomore year. We had a very toxic relationship. Anyway, two months after that Christmas, I found out that they were cheating. Apparently, it had been going on since the beginning of that semester. I thought my relationship was finally in a good place, boy was I wrong." "I'm so sorry, Lou." Carlos put her hand against his cheek. Louise smiled at him, using her nickname. She didn't let anyone but family and her closest friends use that name. "What?" Carlos asked when he looked at her smile.

"Nothing. Everything has turned out for the better. If that didn't happen, then I might not be sitting here with you."

Carlos smiled her smile. "So, this won't be the worse Christmas of your life?" He slyly smiled while kissing her palm. She pulled her hand from his. Ice began worming its way through her heart. She felt the pricks of tears wanting to enter her eyes. She couldn't put the real conversation off anymore.

"What's wrong?" Carlos asked as his face showed worry. The server showed up with their food, giving her a moment to breathe through her fear. Carlos grasped her hand when the server walked away.

"Lou, what's the matter? Did I say something wrong?"

Louise shook her head. "You have been perfect. Every moment of us together has been perfect. But we have been ignoring the bright flashing elephant in the room."

She looked into his eyes. Carlos broke their gaze and looked at his plate. He was going to make her say it.

"Carlos, when are you leaving?"

"I was supposed to leave yesterday."

"And now?"

"I moved my ticket to Christmas morning. I can catch the red-eye and still be home for Christmas morning. I, unlike you, have spent quite a few holidays away from my family. But this one my brother begged me to be there. I think his wife is pregnant again and they want to tell the family together."

Louise nodded and pulled her hand from his to her lap.

"But if it wasn't for that, I would stay."

"Then what?" she asked.

"What do you mean?"

"If you could've stayed a few extra days, you still would have to leave. Carlos, your life is in California. My life is here. This thing has always had an expiration date on it."

"I know." He looked at her. He then slid his arm to her with his palm up. She put her hand back into his. They sat like this for a while before either could say something.

"Our food is getting cold." Carlos finally said.

"I'm not hungry anymore." Carlos reached for her other hand. She gave it to him. She told her hands to remember this moment. His hands seemed to always radiate warmth. She felt at peace with him.

"Louise, I haven't gotten any sleep since I'd realized how much you mean to me. I want to know what we could be. I don't know how to make that happen, but I also know that I can't leave you. I don't want to make a promise I can't keep, but I promise you I will try to make this work."

"I want us to work, too." Carlos leaned over and kissed her. "I don't know how either, Carlos. You live across the country."

"You're right. I live across the country. But we have a few things going for us. We have a lot of technology. Planes fly, cars drive. Unless we have an apocalypse that destroys all electricity, we are good." Carlos smiled his 100-watt smile. The ice that overtook her melted in a second.

"You will try a long-distance thing?" She wasn't ready to use the R-word. Louise was still trying to figure out if this was only an intense crush.

"Louise, I told you I will do whatever you will allow me. I will call every day and night. We can FaceTime, video chat, or send letters." Louise laughed.

"Write letters?"

"Maybe not a letter. A postcard." He leaned in and kissed her again. The server came up and asked if they wanted to-go containers. She looked at the food, her appetite returning. She grabbed her fork and took a bite out of the food. It was delicious, but lukewarm.

"Yes, please." Carlos responded to the server. He then directed his attention back to Louise. "It is cold?"

"No. It's not hot though."

"Well, how about we take it to your house and warm it up? We can try to finish that movie we have been watching for the past few days." Louise smiled. They tried to watch a movie she had been excited about. But they end up talking until late or making out like two high schoolers. Louise nodded. They could pretend to watch the movie another night in a row.

"Ok, but we have to order desert. And I should get something for Angie since I'm going to make her sit in her room another night."

They made it to her house. Carlos warmed up the food for them and they sat on the couch, eating.

"This is good. Too bad we didn't eat it sooner."

"This is more comfortable, anyway." she said. "So, we are really going to do the long-distance thing? I have seen it not be successful before."

"I have never tried it. But I travel a lot with my job. And I have a lot of vacation time stored up. I want to see every season at Cummings."

Louise smiled. "I would love that. Cummings is beautiful this season of course and you know it's my favorite. But for Valentine's Day we have all these silly events. We do a singles' event with a real Cupid. It's cheesy and cute."

"When I come, neither of us will need that, right?" He smiled.

"Nope, we won't need that. But there is a party. And in the spring the flowers are so beautiful. Our garden is amazing. You can see the Easter egg hunt we have for the kids. It's a whole thing. And then summer..."

"And then fall and winter again. And I will have known you for a year." They smiled at each other. Louise felt pressure and nervousness thinking about making plans with Carlos. She knew that a long-distance relationship is doomed. Carlos's smile helped her determine they would make it.

"And I hope you can come visit me. This sunshine person would love to show you the ocean."

"You know, I've only ever went to the beach once. When I was in school, we visited the gulf coast. That was it. I would love to see the ocean with you."

"Good, it's nothing like seeing the sunrise on the horizon. And I know for sure that you will be there with me because of your relentless need to be up early in the morning, every morning."

She laughed at him. "I can't help it. I get so much done in the morning. I feel renewed and ready to take on the world. You have gotten so little sleep since you have been here, haven't you?" Carlos nodded. Louise put their to-go containers on the table and pulled him close to her. She rested his head on her shoulder. "Get some rest." He leaned into her.

Her alarm woke them up the next morning. Louise smiled as she felt Carlos's arms around her. They snuggled on her couch. She was grateful that it was extra-wide. She felt him take a deep breath into her hair as she reached for her phone.

"You can't possibly get up this early," he said. She could hear the smile in his voice. "I have to make breakfast. I usually do meditation and read a little in the morning. I also do some yoga. I have a very busy morning."

Carlos squeezed Louise tighter to him. "Five more minutes."

Louise closed her eyes and snuggled into him. Twenty minutes later, her second alarm went off. This time, she jumped up from the couch. She was still in her date clothes from the night before.

"Carlos, get up. I need to get dressed." Carlos stumbled up from the couch. He looked exhausted. "How about you go back to your room and sleep in? You have nothing to prove to me."

His eyes were still closed. Carlos slowly opened one eye, and to Louise, it sparkled.

"Are you trying to get rid of me, Ms. Cummings?" Carlos's voice was deep with sleep. That inferno that Louise was constantly living with the past few days revved up.

"No. But I also don't need you in the way. We have a lot to finish for the ball tomorrow." Carlos nodded. "Ok, I'll see you around lunch." He pulled her in for a tight hug, and he kissed her cheek.

She appreciated he gave her a cheek kiss as they both had morning breath.

CHAPTER 18

LOUISE WAS IN the mirror, fooling with her hair and trying to calm down her nerves. She finished putting the last hairpin in for her half up-do. She started untwisting the twists she put in the night before so that the half of her hair that would be out would have a little texture for the dinner. Her phone began ringing. It was the event planner.

After a brief conversation, Louise was relieved that everything was going to plan. All she needed to do now was to make it to the ballroom. She finished her hair and applied make-up. Angie made it to her door in time.

"You want help with that?" Angie asked.

"Yes, please." Louise laughed. Angie started working on her make-up.

"I'm excited about tonight." Angie said.

"Yeah."

"I was thinking back to our sleepovers on Christmas Eve. Pretending to want to wait for Santa together. We wanted to sneak down to see everyone dressed their best, watching them dance. It always felt like a fairy tale."

"We were so excited to grow up and be able to go ourselves." Louise agreed.

"All these years and you get your fairy tale night."

Louise absentmindedly nodded. Her fairy tale will be short-lived, as Carlos would need to get to bed early. He would fly out on the red-eye so he could spend Christmas with his family. Louise would spend the next day having their annual Christmas brunch with Jamal and Silas, then dinner with her parents. The sadness that tried to overwhelm her was crushing. Angie paused.

"Sweetie, I'm almost done. Don't mess your face." Louise tried to smile, but the tears building at the back of her eyes wanted to take over.

"Lou. It will be alright. Long-distance relationships can work." Angie tried to comfort Louise. They both knew the truth in that statement. Louise was happy that Angie was so positive, but they both knew the struggle it took to make a long-distance relationship work. Angie tried to maintain one for three years. But resentments would build, and they would place blame. Louise knew that before Carlos left, she would have to break their almost relationship.

"You are right." Louise said. For the next few hours, she would lie to herself.

It didn't take them long to finish dressing. Angie had her bags by the door. She would go with her parents to spend the rest of her vacation with them. Louise was happy to share her best friend with her family, but her house would feel very empty without her. There was another reason her house would be empty, but she refused to think about that right now.

"That should be my dad," Angie said when they heard a horn honk outside. "Do me a favor? Be dramatic."

Louise looked at her, confused, then her doorbell rang. By her phone's camera it was Carlos. She went to open the door, but Angie stopped her.

"Be dramatic! Go upstairs. I'll let him in. I wish I could see his face." Angie winked. Louise followed her orders.

She waited a minute after the door closed to begin her descent. The dress that Louise chose for tonight was an ice-blue mermaid dress. It complimented her curves. It had drop sleeves, so Angie convinced her to put on shimmering lotion. She felt like she glowed. As she descended the stairs, she was awestruck by how handsome Carlos was.

He had on a simple black tuxedo, but it fitted him like they created the suit for him. She saw his intake of breath as he caught sight of her. He slowly let the breath out and smiled at her smile. She smiled back at him. He moved to the steps and reached for her hand as she got to the last one. His kissed her hand.

"You are beautiful," he said.

"You clean up pretty good yourself." She responded.

"You know, we can have our own celebration here."

Louise pushed him towards the door. "Don't tempt me. We have been panning for this since August. I have to show up."

Carlos turned and took her into his arms.

"You can be a little late." His mouth turned into the dangerous grin that turned her insides to mush.

"Despite your very sexy mouth, we have to go now." He nodded but started a kiss that she couldn't imagine ever breaking from. He pulled back from her. She felt a cold settled in her heart. She could count on one hand how many more of those moments that she would have.

"Now we can go." He said.

The ballroom was everything she wanted. It gave the sense of being in an ice castle without the cold. The event planner pulled her away to tour the space. They were ready to open the doors to the waiting crowd. As people trickled in, Louise enjoyed seeing their responses to the ballroom.

The night started out with a formal dinner. Louise had nerves because at her table were Jamal and Silas, who knew about her and Carlos. But her parents, uncle, and aunt would also be there. They were still under the belief that Carlos was working for the estate. She didn't want to have to pretend through dinner that they were only business associates. She had so little time with him.

Carlos decided for them to be out as a couple. As soon as they sat down for dinner, he kissed her cheek. It was a quick peck, but her mother gave her a knowing look. Her mother gestured to the two of them and Louise nodded. Her mother smiled brightly.

The dinner went smoothly despite Louise's stiffness whenever Carlos showed affection. He had a great conversation with her family. She knew that her mother approved. Her father approved of Carlos when he was only consulting. Louise couldn't tell if he approved of boyfriend Carlos. Louise reminded herself that these points were moot, as Carlos would be gone in a few hours.

As they finished dinner, Carlos took her hand. Louise felt her heart implode. She told Jamal that this would be bad for her. Staring into Carlos' eyes let her know it would take months to get over something that only took days to start.

Jamal excused himself from the table and left out of the kitchen door. Louise thought it was strange that he left this way. She was about to follow but found the event planner. She assured Louise that everything was fine and that the band would start soon. Louise's gut told her something was up. She ignored it so that she wouldn't miss anymore moments with Carlos.

Carlos stepped up behind her and hugged her waist.

"I want to be patient. I want to ask you to dance, but if you have to work, I will wait." Louise turned in his arms and looked up at him. Her smile was on his face, and she grabbed his lapels and brought him in for a kiss.

"I'm free. Let's go." She held his hand, and he walked them to the dance floor. The band started with a slow song. Louise requested mostly slow songs for the evening. She knew that she only wanted to be in Carlos's arms and didn't want to be a spectacle like at the club.

Carlos had his arm around her shoulders. It allowed Louise to snuggle into him. Louise rested her head on Carlos' chest. They swayed to the rhythm of the song. Louise smiled to herself. She had never been so contented. Being in Carlos' arms was the only place she ever wanted to be in. They talked about how to make this work. Louise wanted to make it work, so she told herself that it would. She looked up at him.

"We are going to make it. Right?" She said to him. He stopped moving for a second. Then he kissed her.

"We are going to make it."

The song turned more upbeat. Carlos broke from her and walked her to where they kept the coats. After putting on their coats, he walked them outside. The tree was lit for the night and a dusting of snow was on the ground, creating a beautiful scene that complemented the ballroom. They stood at the edge of the veranda, looking out at the tree. Louise let herself imagine doing this with Carlos every year from now on. Her heart swelled as it still tore from the pain of his leaving.

"This was totally unexpected for me, you know." Carlos said. Louise looked up at him. "You are a complete surprise-the most amazing surprise. I thought this would be like every other job."

"Do you flirt with all your other female clients?" Louise bumped into him, trying to turn her serious tone playful. She hated that the question slipped out. Carlos looked at her. He put his hand on her cheek.

"This has never happened to me. You know I flirt but would never cross that line. But you ... this isn't something I normally do. I don't date my clients." Louise let out a breath she didn't know she was holding. She was relieved to know that she wasn't another conquest of Carlos.

"I was afraid," she admitted, "that this was your norm. I haven't been serious about anyone in a long time. Not since I was in school. This was a surprise for me, too."

"I'm not going to tell you I have led a chaste life. I want to be honest about who I am to you. I date a lot. I have a couple of ladies that I can call when needed. But I also haven't been in a serious relationship in a long time. I met my last girlfriend in high school, and we were together for eight years."

"What happened? I'm sorry, I shouldn't have asked that. That is like a fifth date question." Louise tried to back-peddle, but Carlos laughed and hugged her close to him.

"Louise, we are way past that point." He sighed before continuing. "We grew apart. It was sad and took a while for me to get over. When I started with Willis and Spencer, I only wanted a job. I tried my hand at being an entrepreneur before that and the business failed. I was in a lot of debt and needed to take care of myself. We were living with my folks, and I had to get a job to get us our own place again. Well, like I said, I liked the company and wanted to advance. I needed to go back to school to get a college degree for the position I was looking at. That took money, even with the scholarships I had, to fund that dream.

"I told Jen that we needed to save money and stay with my parents for a little longer. She didn't want that, of course. We fought a lot. She wanted me to work so we could build our lives. To her, college wasn't necessary. I was growing in one direction and she in another. So, we broke up. It was a rough period for me. I lost my relationship and business within a year. And was living with my parents. It took a while for me to get back on my feet and to get back to the confidence that you fell in love with the moment you saw me."

He laughed while Louise rolled her eyes. Carlos leaned his chin on top of her head. He exhaled.

"I didn't think that I would find another person I would want to share my life with. I didn't trust that another woman wouldn't demand for me to give up my dreams to be with her." Louise lifted her face to him. Carlos continued, "You are the first person who I have wanted to share all of my dreams with."

She hugged him, knowing she wouldn't be able to let him go.

"Your turn to bare your soul." She felt his laughter rumble in his chest. She pulled back from him with a sly smile.

"I don't know, Mr. Hernández. Are you ready for my soul?"

"I'm ready for whatever you will give me." Carlos's eyes were intense as he stared at her. He leaned in and kissed her. Number two, she thought. The peck at the table didn't count. This was the second kiss before he left her. He kissed every part of her face and neck. It was like his lips were trying to capture her for their memory. She unbuttoned his suit jacket and slid her arms around his back. She felt his laugh again.

"We are outside of the ballroom and your parents are through that door." he said. She started giggling.

"You do know my room number." He went in for kiss number three. "And this sunshine person is very cold."

Louise broke from their kiss and pulled him back to the ballroom. When they walked through the door, she saw Jamal near the back, looking around the room. She headed in his direction, remembering that he left suddenly. He found her in the crowd and started walking toward her. When he reached her, he grasped her free hand and pulled her to the door.

"I need to talk to you." He looked over to Carlos then said, "alone."

Carlos dropped her arm, looking as confused as Louise felt.

"What's going on?" she asked Jamal. Jamal said nothing but continued to walk Louise out of the ballroom and to the administrative hall. He pulled her to his office and closed the door.

"Jay, what's wrong? Is it Si?" Louise looked around. She didn't see who was still in the ballroom before they left. "Are my parents, ok?"

He sat down on the chair in front of his desk and motioned her to sit opposite from him. She didn't move from her position.

"Everyone is ok Lou. Please sit." She went to the chair and sat down, her stomach in knots. Jamal cleared his throat.

"When you came to my house, I thought I better look some more into Carlos. We could tell that you were falling fast, and I wanted to make sure he was worth your time."

"Jay!"

"I know, Lou. I crossed the line. Silas has been mad at me for the past few days. But I had to make sure that you were safe. I wanted to protect you."

"You wouldn't have brought me here if you didn't find out something. What is it? He's married, isn't he. Or engaged or something?"

"No, it's worse." Jamal shook his head.

"Jay, what is worse than him being married? Is he married to several women?" Louise asked.

"It's about the estate." Louise froze at Jamal's words. He closed his eyes, then hung his head. "They have been lying to us. Carlos' company doesn't consult, they also are in acquisitions."

Louise shook her head, not understanding what Jamal was saying. "What does that have to do with the estate?"

"Carlos is here to consult, and the recommendations are for the improvements that his company will make when they buy the estate."

Louise caught her breath. She had no plans of ever selling Cummings. Why would Carlos's company try to buy it? "Jay, I don't get it. We aren't selling the estate."

"We aren't. Malcolm is. He is selling his shares in the estate to Carlos's company. This 'consultation' was so the company can get more information about the estate for the offer that they made to Malcolm. He has been buying up shares from the non-voting family members in secret. By the time we had our spring meeting, he would have sold, and the new company would come in with their ideas."

"How...wha...how did you find out?"

"I had some friends look into Carlos. He is clean as far as the relationship thing. But my friend noticed some similarities on jobs he has been on. When he goes into these small family-owned companies, not long after, Willis and Spencer own them. My friend spoke with the previous owners of one company. Willis and Spencer promised they would grow the company once they bought them out, pushing it into the future—sounds familiar, right? But after the purchase, Willis and Spencer dissolved the business. Apparently, this is what they do. That is the plan for Cummings."

"He lied to me." Louise's heart shredded now. Jamal nodded. "He lied to all of us."

"What about Malcolm? Does he know?"

"I spoke with Malcolm." Jamal had malice in his voice when he said his brother's name. "Malcolm is familiar with how they do business. But the pay day is supposed to be well worth it."

"Who cares about the money? This is our legacy. If this was so beneficial, why not tell the board?"

"Malcolm doesn't care about legacy. And that is exactly what I asked. He said that the board wouldn't get it until he presented Willis and Spencer after they owned his shares. Then they would see the bottom line. Grandmother would see the bottom line is what he didn't say." Jamal blew out a breath. He looked at Louise.

"I'm so sorry." Jamal leaned over and put his hand on Louise's shoulder. She put her hand on top of his and shook her head.

"You didn't do anything. Don't be sorry. Carlos will have to answer for this. And Malcolm. I can't believe this. We must have an emergency meeting. We can't let him sell. There must be some way to stop him. Let's go tell our dads. I will call Uncle Frank."

Louise dragged herself out of her seat. She felt weariness to her core. This will be a long night and she needed to lie in her bed. Jamal finally stood. He nodded his head with a faraway look in his eyes. Louise hugged him.

"I'm so sorry Lou." He said into her hair. Louise felt very inadequate in her dress suddenly. She was in business mode now. She had to save her precious estate. She pulled away from Jamal, pulled her determination up, and squared her shoulders.

"Looks like our Christmas will be a long one." Louise walked to the door. "Come on, we have work to do."

CHAPTER 19

L OUISE WALKED OUT of Jamal's office, and Carlos was leaning against the wall. Louise's fury flamed. Thankfully, that fury hid the pain of her continuously breaking heart.

"Is everything ok?" Carlos asked. There was a hand on her arm. She shook off Jamal's hand and pointed to her office.

She started towards her office and went in. She heard Carlos's hesitant steps coming down the hall. She took a deep breath. Louise didn't want her emotions to take over in this moment. She wanted to send him on his way. She shoved the dread and the pain deep in a closet and turned around to him at her door. For three seconds, she looked into his eyes. She would only allow herself that quick look. The part of Louise that still was falling for this man took a snapshot of his eyes. She remembered how those eyes lavished on her, making her feel alive and special. His eyes wore concern and worry at this moment, and she looked away. Louise focused on Carlos's shoulder. She stepped back and leaned against her desk.

"Lou, are you ok? What is going on?"

"Don't call me that." she whispered. All the hurt she had in her heart spilled from her lips. Carlos was to her in two steps. He reached for her arm, but she yanked it back out of his reach.

"You lied to me." She cleared her throat, reaching for her willpower. "You *lied to us.*"

She looked up into his face, but she couldn't reach his eyes. She rested on his nose where earlier this evening she was kissing. Her broken heart wrung with pain again.

"What are you talking about, Louise?" Carlos stepped closer to her, his arms hovering near her waist. She felt his warmth and wanted to go back in time twenty minutes. She would've stayed on the veranda with him. She would've avoided the ballroom and walked with him to his room. She would've listened to every story he had to give her. It was too late now. She slid past him and stood by the side of her desk.

"Willis and Spencer is planning to buy Cummings from Malcolm." She watched his face as it cringed. Her pain intensified as he contorted his face, revealing that her statement was true.

"I can explain Louise. Let me explain." He started for her again, but she went behind her desk, shaking her head against him.

"Don't you ever touch me."

"I'm sorry. Please let me explain."

"Explain what? You can't explain that you didn't know what was going on. I can see that you knew about this!" Louise hoped Carlos didn't know about the sale. She wanted him to tell her she was wrong. She wanted him to have an explanation that would heal her shattered heart.

"Louise. It's not that simple. I couldn't divulge that part of the deal. I hoped Malcolm would let you know. I had to do my job."

"That's it?" Louise asked, with bitterness seeping from her words. "That is the explanation?"

"Louise..."

"Stop calling me that! Stop saying my name." Louise cut him off. She was being dramatic but hearing her name from his mouth intensified the pain each time he said it. She took a deep breath and continued. "You knew that this sale was happening behind my back, but you didn't tell me. You couldn't divulge the information? You know what this place means to me, what my job means to me, but you keep this enormous secret. How could you?"

"I promise you, I wanted to tell you. I couldn't risk my job." Carlos leaned over the desk, trying to reach for her. Louise crossed her arms.

"You wanted to tell me, but you didn't. We have spent hours together. You talked about the issue with your job. That was the perfect opportunity to tell me. Was anyone of this real?" Her voice faltered at the end as tears welled in her eyes. She looked to the ceiling, willing her eyes not to shed the pain she had been feeling.

"Please, L—", he stopped himself from saying her name. "I'm so sorry. Yes, this is real. The way I feel about you is very real, and I know what you feel is real. Please don't let this one thing destroy us."

"Don't let this one thing—did you really say that? This estate is a 'thing' to you? This is my life! This is my legacy, and you call it a thing? *You lied to me.* You looked me in the face as I shared my dreams of the estate. You sat in that chair, helping me and Jamal come up with a plan to improve the estate. All the while, for what? What plans did your company have?"

Carlos stared at Louise. He looked helpless and defeated. A part of Louise wanted to reach out, but she couldn't. She couldn't deal with a lie.

"Well?" she asked. Carlos stood back and slumped into his chair. He ran his hand through his hair and let out a long breath. He was looking at the floor when he began.

"I told you that I didn't agree with everything about my company. They...we merge with smaller companies. Often, folding the company into our corporate culture. It's presented as an investment into the smaller company but really, they lose what made them a good business.

"Initially Willis and Spencer looked at Cummings Estate as a small boutique hotel. When I got here and saw the estate, of course, I learned that wasn't true. There is so much value in the structure and the land. Your family manages this estate very well. But partnering with you isn't what my company does. When I presented your expansion plan, they loved it. I'm pretty sure they would want to keep you on as manager." Carlos took another deep breath and brought his hands together. He rested his forehead on his knuckles.

"Even though they loved your plan, they still want to tear this structure down to build a larger hotel." Carlos looked back up at Louise. She took a step back, as if someone punched her in the chest.

"Get out!" she exclaimed. Carlos jumped up.

"Please." he begged. Louise shook her head and stepped back, bumping against the wall. She needed its support.

"Go! The bellman should be able to get you a cab to the airport. I want you off my estate in twenty minutes."

"No, we have to talk about this."

"If you are still here in twenty minutes, I will call security to escort you out." She stared at him; this time focused on his cheek. She didn't want to see how hurt he was. Carlos finally turned and walked out of her office. Louise released the breath she was holding and sat in her chair. She texted Jamal to get a cab and security if he wasn't in the lobby in twenty minutes.

> **JAMAL:** I'll handle it. Do you want me to come back there?

LOUISE: No, text me when he is gone.

Fifteen minutes later, Jamal texted he was in a cab heading to the airport. Louise felt the shudders in her chest as the tears she had been controlling finally found their release. One tear slipped out before she heard footsteps coming down the hall. She wiped the tear away and straightened her face to portray calm. Jamal, his parents, and her parents crowded into her office.

"Is this true, Sweetie?" her dad asked. Louise nodded.

"I spoke with . . . Mr. Hernández. It's worse than what Jamal found out. they actually want to build a flashy new hotel, tearing down this building to do so."

"I'm going to call Frank and Mother." Uncle James said. He stepped out of the office to call.

"You can use my office, dad." Jamal said. He mouthed "are you alright? " She nodded. Her mother came around the desk and held her arms out for an embrace.

"Mom, I'm alright." She didn't stand. Louise was not ready for her floodgates to be open. Her mom leaned in close.

"Are you sure, honey?" she whispered. She looked at her mom. She shook her head.

"Let's make it through tonight, ok?"

A COUPLE OF hours later, the family had a solid plan for the next few steps. They would have an emergency board meeting a couple of days after Christmas. Most of the family could get to the estate over the next couple of days so that they can meet before the meeting. Uncle James got in touch with the family lawyer to look up legal precedence for blocking the sale. Louise felt hopeful that they could save the estate.

Louise watched her parents then Jamal drive away. She indulged her mother in a long hug. Louise was proud that she could hold it together. She walked the path to her home knowing that she could finally let the almost girlfriend part of her grieve. As she entered the front door, all the lights were on. Harper and Angie came out of the dining room. Harper held a bottle of tequila. Louise broke down and her friends surrounded her.

The next morning, Louise woke up in her bed fully clothed with a pounding headache. Harper was next to her, still snoring slightly, and she felt Angie behind her. She tried to slide quickly out of the bed, but Angie was awake looking at her phone.

"Harp is going to be out for a while." She whispered. "You want some coffee?"

Louise nodded, then went to the bathroom. Her eyes were puffy from crying most of the night. She tried to wash the residue of her shattered heart away.

Louise met Angie in the kitchen. Angie already had a cup of coffee waiting for Louise. Louise grabbed the cup and placed it on her cheek.

"You want an aspirin, too?" Louise nodded.

"How are you so chipper?" Louise asked.

"I started taking water shots after the third round. I knew you would need a calm head. Thank goodness because I stopped you and Harper from texting Carlos a string of expletives."

Louise grimaced. She didn't remember that. Angie walked to a cabinet and pulled Louise's phone from a top shelf.

"Here. No regret texts went out last night."

"Did we get that bad?"

"Harper did, of course. But you got regretful." Angie's eyebrow raised.

"What does that mean?"

"You were ready to text him to come back,"

Louise didn't remember that. If she had any drunken thoughts about calling Carlos Hernández, she would swear off tequila for real this time. She had texts and missed calls from various family members. She scrolled through her messages until she found the ones she wanted. Carlos sent her quite a few texts. She went to his contact and changed his name to DON'T ANSWER. She then hovered her finger over the block caller button. She closed the phone and put is down on the counter.

"What did he say?" Angie asked.

"I didn't read them. I should block him, right?"

"If you feel that is the best thing to do." Angie said, then took a sip of her coffee. Louise looked at her.

"That didn't answer my question."

"I really don't know what you should do, sweetie. You are hurt right now, so maybe you should block him. Especially if that keeps you from trying to contact him after another drunken night.

"Ok, you are right; I will block him." She opened her phone back up, went to Carlos's contact, and hovered over the block button. She hesitated for another minute or two.

"You are unsure." Angie said, and Louise nodded. "Lou, I think you still need closure. That's probably why you are hesitating. You can block him for now but keep the contact. I think you will need to talk to him, eventually. He ruined things by lying to you, and you need to deal with that. You possibly need to talk to him when you are calm and explain that."

"I can't talk to him again."

"That is how you feel right now. You may change your mind. But having messages from him won't help you be able to do that right now."

Louise agreed. She finally hit the block on his contact. She changed the contact back to his name.

Louise went back upstairs to shower and change into some clothes. She still had a busy day ahead of her, trying to get the meeting together.

LOUISE MADE IT back to her office that afternoon. She checked her phone and responded to the different text messages she had received from her family. Her dad and Uncle James headed back to the hotel so that they could strategize with their lawyer. Their lawyer was still out of town, so they would have to connect remotely.

Jamal walked into her office about thirty minutes after she settled in. "Hi boo, how are you doing today?"

"I'm good. I have everything set up and ready to go. Our dads should be here in about twenty minutes."

"Good. I'm ready. So, now can I talk to my cousin?" Jamal's eyebrows raised. Louise knew she had to have this conversation with Jamal, but she didn't think her heart could take anymore.

"Maybe. Your cousin is tired. She isn't ready to get into it."

Jamal reached over and held her hand. "Lou, I'm so sorry. I hate that I had to be the messenger. Carlos was supposed to be a good guy. He isn't a bad person. But he lied to you. I don't think I can forgive that."

"You and me both. I told him about my last major heartbreak. That should have been the moment that he told me the truth. Any moment could have been the moment. I'm scared for the estate and what all of this could mean. But I'm deeply hurt. We made so many promises to each other. We had 'the talk' and we were going to make it. But now..."

Jamal got up and came around her desk and brought her into an embrace. She let him hug her. She held back the tears, though. She wanted the big cry for when she was finally alone. After a few minutes, he stepped back and held her at arm's length. He looked around her face as if he was looking for something.

"You are going to make it through this." Jamal let go, then leaned against her desk. "Silas has all kinds of plans for cheering you up. He is working on his patented heartbreak care package now."

"As long as said care package doesn't include alcohol, I'm good."

"So, Harper showed up last night?" Louise nodded and Jamal laughed. "How bad is it?"

"My eyelashes were hurting this morning. Thank goodness, Ang didn't drink as much as us. She stopped us from doing anything stupid and regretful."

"I'm glad about that. So, have you talked to him?"

Louise shook her head and stared at her computer.

"That's for the best, I guess," Jamal said.

"Ang said I need closure." Louise used her fingers as quotation marks.

"I don't think you do."

"Me either. And anyway, we are too old to pull the tricks you made me do for you to get closure. I also don't want to get arrested...again."

Jamal cackled. "You know that was your fault. I said run, but you wanted to stay and finish the tires. When I say run, we run."

Louise joined in the laughter. She was glad that Jamal started laughing at his old heartbreaks. Maybe she would one day.

Their fathers walked in while they were still laughing.

"Hey sweetheart. You both look like you are in good spirits. Any good news?" her dad inquired.

"No, Daddy. We were reminiscing about our younger, dumber days. We made it out of those, and we can make it out of this." She answered.

"That is true, sweetie. I mean, when Sheriff Coles called me to say you were in jail for vandalism. And Jamal was trying to bail you out with $27.35...that was an interesting time."

Jamal and Louise started laughing again. "That is the example I used."

"I know we will make it through this," her dad replied. Uncle James sat down in the chair. Louise felt a tug at her heart, knowing who the chair now belonged to. She would order new office furniture tonight.

"I plan to call Malcolm after this meeting. I will tell him about the emergency board meeting and get him to come. Mother will be here this evening and Walt early in the morning." Uncle James said, pulling them back into the current situation. Louise pulled her monitor around so that everyone could see it.

"Alright, let's get this meeting started then." she said.

Louise finally made it back to her house late that evening. She made Harper and Angie go to be with their families. Louise needed to release fully before going into the meeting. She had one more day to prep, and she wanted her mind fully focused on what she needed to do for the estate. Tonight, she could hash out her feelings for the man. She went to her fridge, and it was full of Christmas dinner leftovers. Her mom had been to the house and stuffed her fridge. She pulled out the food and warmed it up. As the food was warming, she started scrolling through her phone.

Louise hated notifications looming at her, so she kept going to her messages in-between looking at her social media pages. She tried to ignore the unread message. She headed to her couch when the food was warm and turned on her TV. Her screen was still on the movie that she and Carlos were trying to watch for days. She felt the pressure in her chest as the pain finally seeped out. She grabbed a pillow and released the tears.

Louise sat like that for what felt like hours, but her phone in her hand said twenty minutes. She wiped the last of the tears away. She pulled her knees to her chest and geared up to read the texts she had avoided.

> **CARLOS:** Louise, please answer. Let me explain.

> **CARLOS:** I'm so sorry. I didn't mean for this to happen.

> **CARLOS:** Louise, please. I'm sorry. I should have told you everything.

> **CARLOS:** Answer my call please.

> **CARLOS:** Louise. please…

Another round of crying ensued as Louise read through his text messages. She considered unblocking his number and calling him to talk. She wanted to hear his voice one more time. Her better self reminded her of why that would be a bad idea. He still lied. He still misled her for days. She wasn't ready to forgive him. It struck her how short everything was with him. In a few weeks, she let this man come into her life and her heart. Louise knew she was stronger than this. She wouldn't let this heartbreak be the end for her. She let a man stop her from loving before, and she wouldn't again.

Louise wiped all the tears away and blew her nose one last time. She wouldn't cry over Carlos Hernández any longer. He stole enough of her time. Louise got up and started cleaning the house. She could still smell his cologne on her couch. She would rid Carlos Hernández from her life. She cleaned and sprayed deodorizer on the couch. She vacuumed her rugs and mopped the floor. When she finished, her living area smelled like lemon and pine.

Louise then started in her kitchen. She first trashed the apron that she put on him. Then she wiped down the counters and swept and mopped the floor. Last, she went into the dining room and repeated the steps of cleaning. Now that her downstairs was back to pre-Carlos, she felt in control. Even though Carlos Hernández never made his way upstairs, Louise headed up there to finish cleaning. She cleaned and washed until it was two in the morning.

Louise rose at her normal time and did her usual routine. She was out of her house at her normal time, walking up to the estate. She entered the doors and looked up at the ceiling. After a few seconds, she looked over to his chair, a part of her expecting him to be waiting for her. It was empty the way it should have been. Louise stepped to the chair and slid it closer to the fireplace. The area looked empty, but she wanted it that way. She turned to the front desk person, waved, then marched to her office. Louise then took the chairs and sat them on the outside of her office. She spent the morning ordering new furniture for delivery after the first of the year.

Louise had maintenance remove the old chairs and sent a message to have anybody claim them. She sat back and felt the control return that she let go of days ago. She let her heart run things when it came to Carlos Hernández. For her next romance, she would lead with both her head and her heart. Obviously, she couldn't trust her heart anymore.

CHAPTER 20

THE DAY OF the meeting arrived. Louise felt stronger and ready to handle their dealings with Malcolm. The estate didn't have any provisions in place to stop him from selling his shares, but the family was sure that they could convince him not to sell. Louise and Jamal agreed they didn't care why Malcolm wanted to sell, but the rest of the family wanted to hear him out. They hoped Malcolm would listen to reason.

When Louise arrived at the estate that morning, and after looking at the ceiling, she looked over at the empty spot. She knew that, for aesthetics, she needed to put something there. For now, she was fine with the emptiness.

The night before, she got a call from Grandmother to meet her in the dining room when she arrived at work. She felt fortified for the meeting with the family, not so much for meeting with Grandmother. Louise headed to the dining room, and Grandmother was there. She had on a dark suit and her hair pulled back in a bun. She sat straight-backed and proud; she was always regal to Louise. It struck Louise how much she favored her grandmother. They both had on dark blue; hair similar with little makeup. Louise had always felt they differed completely from how they approached the running of the estate, but Grandmother loved Cummings the same, if not more than Louise. Grandmother would be Louise's best bet to make sure that Cummings stayed in the family.

"Good morning, Grandmother."

"Good morning, Louise. Please sit. Would you like something?"

"No ma'am. I ate at home." Grandmother pursed her lips in disapproval. Louise cleared her throat and continued. "I'm sure you want to talk about today's meeting. Since we found out everything, I haven't been able to speak to you directly.

"I don't really want to talk about the meeting. Your father and James have kept me informed of everything. I trust the direction that you all want to take today in dealing with Malcolm."

Louise nodded; her curiosity piqued.

"I want to know how you feel about running Cummings." Grandmother retorted.

"I don't understand?"

"Louise, all you have ever known has been the Cummings Estate. I did not expect you to take over, but you did. When Frank wanted to step down to pursue other interests, your father was running the charity so seamlessly, and Malcolm was in California. I felt Jamal could take over, but he said no. Cummings then fell into your lap."

"I don't see it that way, Grandmother. I spent most of my life learning every part of the business. All I ever wanted was to work here at the estate. I know nothing else. I don't want to know anything else. I love the Cummings."

Louise took a deep breath, asking the question she always had in the back of her mind but feared to ask. "Are you dissatisfied with my management? Would you rather Jamal take the lead?"

Louise looked down at the table. She had her hands wringing under the table.

"Louise." Louise looked up at grandmother. "I asked because I didn't want you burdened with running the estate. James and your father said that it was their responsibility to run this place. Frank wanted to go into construction. When it came to my grandchildren, I didn't want you to feel responsible for the Cummings estate. I want you all to be here, to do this out of love. I think you are doing an amazing job running Cummings. I won't lie to you—I wanted Malcolm to run the estate. His being named after your grandfather always lead me to believe that he would be a superb manager. But you have your grandfather's spirit and excitement for Cummings. And a little of my common sense.

"Louise, I never questioned you running Cummings. I didn't want to burden you with it."

Louise felt the tears slip from her eyes. "Oh Grandmother. I never felt burdened by Cummings. This is the only place I feel at peace."

Louise jumped up and hugged her grandmother. She felt Grandmother's grip tighten, but she quickly let go. She heard Grandmother grunt, then Louise let go. Grandmother came from a generation when you weren't overly sentimental. Grandmother never was much for hugs and kisses. Louise sat back down in her seat.

"Now that we got that cleared up, tell me about the consultant. His name was..." Grandmother said.

"Carlos." Louise felt her heart tug at saying his name.

"Yes, Carlos Hernández. You worked the closest with him. Tell me about him. Was there really no indication of how the company works?"

Louise took a deep breath and cleared her throat. She wasn't ready to rehash anything dealing with Carlos Hernández.

"No, there wasn't. He rarely spoke about his company. He came in and observed, then sent the report."

"Yes, that report was very thorough. He identified some big pain points. I was very impressed by the second report of recommendations. You and Jamal did an excellent job with that."

"Thank you. But he helped." Louise took another deep breath. "Mr. Hernández."

"I could tell he helped. But I feel the bulk of the decisions were you and Jamal. After reading the report, I feel confident about moving forward with the expansion. It is a good idea, something I know your grandfather would have wanted to do. I think we will vote on that today as well."

Louise's mouth dropped. "Are you serious?"

Grandmother stared at Louise. "Of course, you are serious. Thank you, Grandmother!"

Louise stopped herself from the second hug she wanted to give Grandmother. Instead, they sat in silence for a while.

"Grandmother, how did you know that Grandfather was the one?"

Grandmother leaned her head to the side. She looked confused. But then she had a small smile. "I don't think I ever knew he was the 'one'. In my day, we didn't' look at marriage like that. Your grandfather was a good man, and he wanted to take me away. That's all I knew at the time. When he came to Alabama, he seemed so out of his element. But he was kind to everyone. When he asked me to marry him, my father approved, so I said yes. I had only known him for two weeks. Our first kiss was at our wedding, then I was heading to my new home. We had a wonderful life together, but it wasn't perfect. We stayed together through the hard times and the good."

"I bet he never lied to you."

"Ha!" Louise had never heard her grandmother burst into laughing this loud. "Louise, your grandfather lied a lot. Especially in the beginning."

Louise's mouth was open again, and her eyes were wide.

"Among all of your grandfather's amazing qualities, his confidence was the one thing that attracted me the most. He told my father that he ran a successful estate. Maybe he didn't lie to us as much as he lied to himself. Cummings was struggling when I arrived. And over the years, we had some tough times. Your grandfather didn't always share that with me. That is why I became an expert in the business. I had to know when we weren't doing well because your grandfather wasn't as open with it."

"So, you forgave him?"

"Of course, I did. It wasn't easy, but I loved him. I wasn't the easiest to live with, either. I can be a bit gruff." Grandmother smirked at Louise. "But when you love someone, you work through the difficult times. You forgive them when it's hard."

Grandmother narrowed her eyes at Louise. "Why do you ask?"

"No reason." Louise answered a little too fast. Grandmother still had a suspicious look on her face.

"Well, I hope you won't be like the young people I see giving up all the time. Marriage takes work. And if the person is worth it, and doesn't mean you harm, then you should work on it."

"Thanks, Grandmother. I'm sure if I ever find love, I will heed your words." Louise glanced at her phone. They still had a few hours until the meeting.

"Go, do your work. I will be here waiting for Malcolm. I told him to meet me as soon as he arrived." Grandmother said.

"I would tell you to go easy on him, but I'm still mad at him. So, give him all the He... Heck." Grandmother smiled and shook her head.

"I'll see you in the conference room." Louise said, then headed back to her office.

LOUISE SHOWED UP to the conference room an hour early. She was the only one there, and she used the quiet to steady herself. She felt confident they could talk Malcolm out of selling, or at the least write him a check that would be acceptable. Louise spent yesterday liquidating some of her assets so she could buy Malcolm out of his shares. With that, he wouldn't have to worry about being on the board or deciding about the estate. She closed her eyes to take some deep breaths. She rolled her neck and then opened her eyes. She was ready.

Jamal walked in a few minutes later with Grandmother. Her grandmother uncharacteristically smiled at her. Louise was glad that they had their talk. She now knew that her grandmother was proud of her work with the estate and that helped to build her confidence. Her parents walked in soon after, her mother walking straight to her and hugging her.

"How are you, sweetie?" Her mother whispered.

"I'm good. I'm better every day." Louise gave her mom a small smile.

"You know I'm here for you. You don't have to go through this heartache alone." Her mom said. Louise glanced at her father and grandmother. "Don't worry about your dad. I didn't tell him my suspicions. I wanted you to come to us."

"I do owe you an explanation. Everything happened so fast. I'll come by the house tonight." Louise hugged her mother.

"I'm glad. I miss you. I'll make your favorite meal." Louise smiled and let go. Her uncles and their wives walked into the room. Jamal walked over to her. They still had a few minutes before the meeting was supposed to start, but no hint of Malcolm.

"Have you seen your brother?" Louise asked.

"I had to pick him up at the airport. He had little to say. He said to wait until the meeting to hash everything out. He did finally ask Lynn to marry him. So, that's good news."

"I'm sorry that you can't really celebrate."

"I'm so mad at him. Of all the people he could at least told me. I know we haven't been close in a while, but this isn't right."

Louise rubbed Jamal's arm, knowing that this whole thing hurt him as much as her. She couldn't imagine the betrayal that Jamal felt when he found out the news. She felt bad. She spent the past couple of days trying to heal her broken heart when he was breaking, too.

"How about I come to you house after the meeting? We can talk and hang out. We still haven't had our Christmas." Jamal gave her a sad smile and nodded. She turned to the door at Malcom finally walked into the room. Louise caught her breath as Carlos Hernández walked into the room right behind him. She tightened her grip around Jamal's arm, using him to steady her. Jamal turned and saw what she saw.

"You ok, Lou?" He leaned in and whispered to her. She couldn't stop herself from looking into Carlos's eyes. He looked sad. Louise quickly looked away and told Jamal she was alright. She went to sit in her seat by her mother, who held her hand. Louise held on tightly as she needed something to keep her from displaying the emotion she spent the past day suppressing. Grandmother stood in her place at the head of the table and called the meeting to order. Louise straightened her back and held her head high. This was about the estate, not her personal life. She looked over at grandmother.

"Since this is an emergency meeting," Grandmother started, "we won't do any of the usual business. We are here to clear up this issue of Malcolm selling his shares to the Willis and Spencer firm. Malcolm, I see that you have brought along someone."

"Yes Grandmother, this is Carlos Hernández. He is who came to consult for the firm. He has firsthand knowledge of the status of the estate and the offer that Willis and Spencer have on the table. I thought his opinion would help to clarify and answer questions." Malcolm said.

"It's nice to meet you, Mr. Hernández. I wish it was under better circumstances." Grandmother also nodded at him. Louise refused to look in that direction. She was happy that they were sitting at the opposite end of the table.

"It is my pleasure, Mrs. Cummings. I am sorry that this is the circumstance under which we meet." Carlos said, and Louise's heart grated. She didn't think that her crushed heart could continue to be in pain. She felt several eyes on her. Her mother squeezed her hand. Louise didn't move. She still hoped she looked at regal as she pretended to be.

"Yes. Thank you for coming, but we aren't really interested in hearing the offer that your company made to Malcolm. I am impressed by the report that you made and then the report you and Louise and Jamal came up with for improvements to the estate. So much so that I told Louise this morning that I am ready to vote on the expansion plan that she made at our last board meeting." She heard the intake of breath and the whispers around the table. She snuck a glance at Jamal, who was across the table from her. He was smiling brightly. He mouthed, "Is she serious?" Louise nodded and smiled. Louise relaxed a little and looked around the room. She locked eyes with Carlos Hernández, who had a small smile on his face. She turned back to Grandmother with a frown. She couldn't share this joy with the one person who she wanted to.

"But before we can take that vote, and I have every intention of doing that today, we need to talk with Malcom. Malcolm, we want to give you a chance to explain. You know that the board doesn't support this sale and will do what we need to stop it. But we want to know why you have chosen this path."

Grandmother sat down and motioned for Malcolm to stand

and speak. Louise couldn't look in his direction because she knew where her eyes would go. She heard Malcom clear his throat.

"Grandmother, board members. First, I want to apologize for the deception." Jamal made a loud grunt. "Despite what you all may think, I knew that Mr. Hernández here would've been met with hostility and distance if you all knew why he was here. I have worked with the Willis and Spencer firm for a couple of years now, and I believe in their business. When I made this decision, I couldn't have found a better corporation. Now, I will have Mr. Hernández explain more about his firm."

"Malcolm, that is not what Grandmother asked. She asked why?" Jamal interrupted.

"Yes son, we are sure that Mr. Hernández has a wonderful presentation. But first we would like to know what brought you to the decision to want to sell your shares in Cummings." Uncle James said.

Louise had to see Malcolm's face during his explanation. Malcolm looked uncomfortable. Louise suspected that all the hiding and secrets were because he didn't want to face his family. She looked around the room and many had a look of hurt on their faces. Jamal's face mirrored the anger she wore on hers.

"I, um...Look, coming to this decision wasn't easy for me. I had to look at the bigger picture. I love the Cummings Estate, and it has been in our family for a long time. But like any family dynasty, it eventually would fall into the hands of some other entity. Look at our generation—Louise and Jamal have taken the reins, but I'm sure that Uncle Frank's kids have their own dreams. And I'm now in L.A. and don't plan to return home. So that means any children Lou or Jamal have will take over the estate. It's not fair to make anyone work here. We can partner with this firm for the overall running of the estate. It will still bear our name, and they are offering a generous package for my shares."

"Malcolm," Louise said, "First of all, neither I nor Jamal see the estate as a burden." Louise looked at Jamal, hoping she was right. He always did his job without complaint. She was sure he would tell her if he wanted to leave.

"Lou is correct. This is not a burden."

"Jamal, you always complained about working at the estate. You were the main one that didn't want to be here working in the estate and living in town. You wanted more." Malcolm blurted.

"But then I grew up, Malcolm. My desires changed when I found my love and everything I ever wanted. And he moved here for me. I'm happy. And as far as the estate, I rebelled against working here for many years, but I love Cummings. I want to see every plan Louise has for it. She is the best leader, and I will go wherever she will take us."

Jamal looked over the Louise. They smiled at each other. Louise knew she couldn't have a better partner.

"Well Malcolm, I hope that changed you point of view. Cummings is not a burden to anyone who is sitting in this room. We all have chosen to be here." Grandmother said.

"Are you sure about that? Will any of you be honest, finally? Grandmother, we love you and the dream you and Grandfather had for us, but it was your dream, not ours." Malcolm said.

"Since you brought me up indirectly, I guess it's my turn to speak." Uncle Frank said. "It's true that I am the one who first rebelled against working at the estate. I left Sacamore and didn't look back. But I still have an interest in what happens to Cummings. I don't expect my children to do anything but what makes them happy. I hope they would want to follow in the footsteps of Louise and Jamal, but I won't push. Part of the plans that Louise and I discussed is me helping her find the right company for the construction. We have been talking about moving the family up here for the summer to help in the beginning stages. I want to be more involved with the estate.

"You spoke of the dream that my parents had. It wasn't my dream at first, but my heart would always be here at the estate. I think we all feel that way. Except for maybe you, Malcolm."

Malcolm stared at his hands on the table. "Would you all at least listen to the benefits of a sale?" he asked.

"Yes, Malcolm. You pulled Mr. Hernández from his holiday to talk to us. Mr. Hernández, please tell us how the Willis and Spencer firm could help Cummings Estate," Grandmother said.

Louise force stopped her eyes from looking at him. She stared at Malcolm. Hearing Carlos's voice was hard enough. She refused to continue breaking her own heart.

"I'm sorry, Mrs. Cummings. I can't tell you that." Malcolm shot a look at Carlos. Everyone turned their attention to him.

"Excuse me, Mr. Hernández?" Grandmother asked.

"Mrs. Cummings, unfortunately my company will not partner with you to assist in your plans. My company will purchase the Cummings Estate and follow the plans they have for it. The Willis and Spencer firm is a predatory company. They have plans to turn this into a big resort. This building doesn't play into that plan."

Carlos looked at Louise. She didn't look away. He looked resigned. Her heart wanted to break for him, but she told herself that he was the one in the wrong.

"Mr. Hernández, if Malcolm sells his shares, our board will still be the majority shareholders. How does your company expect to get the rest of us to sell?" Grandmother asked.

"I don't think upper management has a plan in place currently for the rest of you not selling. They will offer a huge amount. The land and the area will be worth it. In the improvement plan, I'm sure you saw how you could bring in a lot of business creating a space for skiing. My company plans would include a ski lodge. So, if you all chose not to sell, I can only imagine that they will make things difficult for you. Possibly buying the land around you and shutting you out. They have done it before." Carlos shrugged.

"Thank you, Mr. Hernández, for your honesty. I expect that sharing this information won't bode well for you." Grandmother said. Carlos hung his head a little in acknowledgement. "But we have much to discuss as a family. If you don't mind, please let us talk."

Carlos nodded and stood. He looked at Louise and she met his gaze. His eyes didn't glow. They were more of a sunset and her heart wrung. How could he still melt and inflame her at the same time? He said before he left.

"For what it's worth, Mrs. Cummings, I would hate it if you all sold this place. It's special. I felt that the moment I walked in. And your family made me feel like home, a sentiment that I heard from many guests while I was here." He directed his words to Grandmother, but his eyes never left Louise. He turned and walked out the door. Louise looked up to the ceiling to hold back the round of tears that tried to fall. When she was back in control, she felt the knowing eyes of Jamal and her parents on her. Even Grandmother had a wispy smile while staring at Louise. Louise cleared her throat.

"Malcolm, you can't sell." Louise said, as she looked over at him. He was looking at his hands, deep in thought. He finally gave her his attention. "Please reconsider this plan. Our legacy is in this estate. I get that you have a life in L.A., and I want you to live it fully. If Cummings feels like a burden to you, I will relieve that burden. I don't know how much Carl—Mr. Hernández's company—is offering you, but I will write you a check right now."

Louise heard the intake in breath by her mother and grand-mother. The whole table turned to her. She hadn't discussed her plan with anyone. She didn't want to get into legal battles or a lot of back and forth. Louise wanted to make sure that Cummings was secure.

"I have $100K liquid right now. Depending on their offer, I can get more. I can call my banker and get a loan for more. What were they offering?" Louise inquired.

"Louise, this was not the plan." Her father said.

"Louise, I can't let you do that." Grandmother said. Louise waved both off, still staring at Malcolm. She couldn't read his cloudy look.

"Tell me the offer and I will increase it by 10%."

Malcolm finally looked at her. He looked defeated. "I won't sell it to them. I only ask for the amount I have spent buying shares from our cousins. This is not how I wanted this to happen."

Linda, Jamal and Malcolm's mom, got up and hugged her son.

"Thank you, Malcolm," Grandmother said. Louise looked at Jamal. He still looked angry.

"Thank you, Malcolm," Louise said. "This estate is our leg-acy, but you are family. I hate you didn't come to us with how you were feeling. No matter what, we are still family, and we love you."

Jamal looked at her and scowled. Louise knew he wanted to be mad a little longer, but she also knew he needed to forgive his brother. She pointed her chin to Malcolm. Jamal got up and went to him, holding his hand out for a shake. Malcolm grabbed his hand but pulled him into a hug. Grandmother touched Louise's arm. She whispered, "thank you."

"Alright, that is enough sentiment. I believe Louise has or-ganized food in the dining room from her chef, and I'm about ready for something. I hope it's American." Grandmother said.

"Don't worry, Grandmother. The sous chef is from North Carolina, and she is making you pot roast, greens, and cornbread." Louise laughed. She felt lighter. She was happy to know that the Cummings would be theirs for another hundred years. The family headed to the dining room. Louise told the group that she wanted to change, so she headed to the lobby. As she rounded the corner, Carlos was sitting in his chair.

CHAPTER 21

L OUISE FROZE. SHE wasn't ready to see him. She needed closure, but she couldn't face him yet. She pulled her
coat tightly across her body and bolted to the front doors.
"Louise!" His voice stopped her in her tracks. She heard his
footsteps as he made his way to her. She wanted to move, but
her heart had control and it waited for him to reach her.

"Can we talk, please?" Louise turned and looked at him.
Stress etched into his face. She wanted to massage the crease
that formed in-between his brows. He reached for her but didn't
touch her. His eyes pleaded for her permission. She stepped back.

"I don't think we have anything to talk about, Ca—
um...thank you for your words. You shouldn't have left your
family for that. But I appreciate them. Malcolm agreed to halt
the deal. Sorry that you came all this way for that. I wish you
a pleasant trip home." She held out her hand, and he put his in
hers. Louise shook his hand, then let go. She turned and hurried
to her house. Behind her door, she cried. This time, she knew it
would be her last time seeing Carlos.

Louise packed a bag and headed to Jamal's house. She would
spend the night in town at her parent's house. After everything

that happened, she earned a couple of days off from the estate. Her mom texted that the family would be there to have a small celebration for Malcom's engagement. Louise was happy for Malcolm and happy that her family was moving on from what he did. Forgiving him felt easy. She wished she could forgive Carlos that easily. If she could, maybe she could finally let him go. For now, her heart was pushing her to call or text him. Her pride kept her from touching her phone, and she was happy that it had control.

Silas answered the door and pulled her in for a long hug. Louise didn't realize how much she needed a Silas hug. He was always so non-judgmental. He didn't demand from her; he let her be. Silas pulled back and looked at her.

"My poor Lou. Come on. I have lots of wine." Louise grimaced. "Come on, you can't still be off alcohol? Ok, well, I have lots of chocolate, too."

Silas pulled her to the couch and went into that kitchen. He came out with a piece of chocolate cake and chocolate ice-cream in a bowl.

"This is a bit much, don't you think?" Louise asked with a smile.

"Nope, I actually think we are missing chocolate syrup and sprinkles. I call it the 'heartbreak special'."

"So, this is the gain of a lot of weight special!"

"Calories don't count when you are nursing a heartbreak. The calories you lose from crying balances the ones you get from eating. How are you doing anyway?"

Louise took a deep breath and put the plate on the table. She pulled one of her legs under her on the couch.

"I don't know, Si. He was at the estate for the meeting."

"Jay mentioned it. How did that go?"

"I didn't think I could hurt anymore. But seeing him and

then having to say goodbye. It was torture." Louise leaned her head on the back of the couch. Silas held her hand.

"Lou, I wish I could fix this for you. Are you sure saying goodbye to him was the right thing? Jamal said that he told the truth about his company and that kind of helped Malcolm come around. Do you think you can forgive him?"

Louise closed her eyes. She wanted to forgive him. She wanted to release herself from this pain that he caused. She was too angry.

"I don't know, Si. I know forgiving him is what I need. But he lied to me. I can't handle someone lying to me. How would I trust he won't lie when we are 3,000 miles away from each other? He had this big lie, and we weren't even together. I don't think that I could pursue a relationship with him. For my sanity, I'm sure that I will have to forgive him, but I won't have to talk to him to do that." Louise explained.

"Sweetie," Silas pulled Louise into a hug, "You will get through this. It will be hard, but you are also one of the strongest people I know. Know that you don't have to be strong for me or Jay. If you need to cry or scream or throw things, we got you. Don't break my stuff. I have these old things of Jay's that we need to throw away."

They both chuckled. Louise was again thankful that Jamal and Silas found each other.

"When I need to break some things, I promise Jay's old junky stuff is first on my list. Can I have my basket now?" Silas's eyes lit up.

"Babe, bring the basket out!" Silas jumped up from the couch as Jamal walked out from the back rooms with an enormous basket. It had all her favorite jams from a local shop and more chocolate. It also has fruits and a bouquet of flowers. Louise beamed when Jamal set it on her lap.

"Thank you, Si! You know how to make a girl feel special."

"Well, you are my favorite girl." Silas put his arm around Louise and pulled her close.

"I swear he only married me to get close to you." Jamal said. Louise stuck out her tongue and snuggled closer to Silas. Jamal was looking at his phone. Louise sat up.

"What's wrong?" she asked. Jamal's brows furrowed, but he cleared his face and smiled at her.

"Nothing. It seems like we are putting off our Christmas again. Silas promised to bring the lasagna he made at your parents' house. And I think you mom wants help cooking some things."

"Yeah, she texted me to be there ASAP and not to eat too much over here. I have your gifts in the car. Si, do you have anything for tomorrow? I'm taking the day off, and Jay, you were going in later anyway, right? Can we do Christmas tomorrow?"

"That is a great idea. I'm free and we can have our brunch. Invite Angie and Harper. I haven't seen Ang at all since she been back." Silas said. Jamal was busy texting on his phone.

"Jay, babe, are you with us?" Silas asked.

"Um, yeah. Christmas tomorrow morning. That will work. Let's get to your parent's house then." Silas and Louise exchanged looks. Jamal was up to something.

The next morning, Louise woke and took a shower to put on another pair of pajamas. This pair she kept in her old room. It was a dark green set with red borders. It had tiny elves and candy canes all over the set. She smiled when she looked at herself in the mirror. She still felt sad about her so-called break-up, but she was happier about the night before.

It had been years since most of her family were together to celebrate. Usually when they saw each other, it was for the board meetings. Malcolm called up his fiancée on FaceTime so they could congratulate them both. Louise even had Grandmother in the kitchen baking Louise's favorite cake. It was a hummingbird cake Grandmother kept the recipe secret to herself. She finally gave it to Louise and walked her through how to make it. Louise felt peaceful.

But a tear still rolled down her face. It was one person the whole night that she wanted to share this joyous occasion with. She sent him away. Looking in the mirror, she started second-guessing herself. Why couldn't she forgive Carlos? Were her walls that she put up from her first major heartbreak, keeping her from trusting him? Shouldn't she be able to forgive a person of one lie? She forgave Malcolm. How hard would it be to forgive Carlos?

She couldn't answer any of these questions right this minute, so she headed downstairs. Louise's mom was in the kitchen making breakfast.

"Morning Mom." She kissed her mom on the cheek.

"Morning Lou-Lou." Her mom smiled at the pert name she used to call her.

"Where are dad and Grandmother?"

"Your grandmother is still in the guest room. I'm sure she is reading her devotional. Your dad is out shoveling the snow. He wanted to make sure you could get out."

Louise looked out the window. It snowed overnight. The backyard looked like a snow globe with the loose snow and icicles formed on the trees. She took a couple of pictures with her phone. She went to her text messages and almost sent the pictures to the number that was now blocked on her phone. Louise sighed and put down her phone.

"What's wrong, dear?"

"Nothing." Louise said, then changed her mind. "Did you ever date anyone besides dad?"

Her mom chuckled. "Of course, I did. I dated a lot before I met your dad."

"A lot mom, gosh!"

"Baby, I was alive in the seventies. I enjoyed myself! Remind me to tell you about my risqué stories from Woodstock." Her mom winked. "Why do you ask?"

"First, yuck! I wondered—did you ever get your heart broken before him?"

Her mom turned off the pan she was frying bacon in and put the cooked bacon on a plate laden with a paper towel. She then motioned for Louise to sit at the table. She made them both a mug of coffee and came to the table and sat across from Louise.

"I've mentioned the boyfriend I had before your dad." Louise nodded. "Well, I never gave you the details about what happened. Me and that boyfriend, John, were together for six years. We moved in together and our families knew each other. We spent holidays and vacations together and I knew we would get married one day. I was content in waiting for him to ask the question. One day he came home, I had cooked dinner, we sat down to eat, and he said we needed to talk. I assumed it was 'the' talk. The talk planning our engagement. I was wrong. He said that he wasn't ready for this commitment and that it was more that he wanted to experience. He would leave in a week to go to Europe. He didn't think it was fair for me to wait for him. I told him I would go with him; I mean who doesn't want to go to Europe? But he said he needed to go alone.

"By alone, he meant that he needed to go with one of his co-workers that I didn't trust. But I didn't find that out until a few months later. It devastated me. I put all my hopes for the future in this one man. We built a life together and he blew it in a fifteen-minute conversation. The part I regret is finishing dinner with him. I should have thrown him out right then." Her mother chuckled.

"Mom, I'm so sorry."

"It was a long time ago. I met your dad here at the estate six months later. But of course, you know that story...boy meets girl, boy falls in love with girl, girl rejects boy and goes back home. Boy follows girl and swears his undying love to her, blah blah blah." Louise smiled. She heard her parents' love story so many times over the years that she could recite it word-for-word with her mom. Her mother was on vacation with some girlfriends at the estate. When her father saw her, he fell in love. Her mother wasn't so easily swayed. They had dinner on her mom's last night at the estate, and her dad said he wanted to marry her. Her mom didn't believe it and left. A week later, her dad showed up at her house with a ring. He pursued her for a year before her mom realized that she too was in love, and they married and have been together ever since.

"What about moving here? You gave up your life to be with dad. Was that easy?"

"It wasn't that hard. I liked my job and my friends, but I loved your father more. I probably would've move to Antarctica if he asked. And you know I hate the cold." They both laughed. Her mother was from Texas and had a hard time adjusting to living in the north.

"I guess the men in our family really love them some southern girls."

"They do," her mom touched her hand. "If you really love someone, you don't think about what you are giving up for them. You do it. I believe that if I really tied my roots to Houston, your dad would have moved for me."

Louise's phone buzzed. Harper texted:

> **HARPER:** I'm on the way. Be ready. I got Ang already. I borrowed Mack's truck. Be outside at five.

"Thanks, Mom. Harper is on the way."

"Ok, be safe and have fun. And grab the box by the door. I got some things for Jamal and Silas. I found some silver decorations that will match their tree. Christmas was different this year."

"Next year we will make it up." Louise reassured her.

"I know you want to be with the young people for New Year's Eve, but me and your daddy wouldn't mind if you came by for a bit," her mother replied.

"I'll see, Mom. Why don't you all come to the estate?"

"I don't want to be around all those folks. Now, go before Harper starts honking." Louise gave her mom a hug and headed to the door. By the time she bundled up and out the door, Harper pulled up in a truck she borrowed from another one of their childhood friends, Mack. She waved at her dad, who was clearing the snow off his car. She felt bad not using her own car as he cleared the snow from there, too.

"Thanks, Dad! And sorry!" He waved her off.

It was a quick trip to Jamal and Silas' house. Harper was quiet, which was unusual for her. When they entered the house, Silas hugged Louise with a huge smile on his face.

"What's up with you?"

"Nothing," he said as he helped her out of her coat and gloves.

"Is Jay in the kitchen? What can I do to help?" Louise asked.

"Nothing. But Harper, can you come squeeze some oranges? Lou Jamal wanted to talk to you in his study. Ang, I love those PJs! You can finish setting the table."

Louise got a very suspicious feeling from Silas. He was extra happy and talkative. And why did Jamal want to talk to her alone? She hoped that he and Malcolm hadn't gotten into another fight. Louise walked over to Jamal's study, knocked, and pushed the door open.

"Jay, please tell me you didn't get into it with Malcolm..." Louise froze. Jamal was sitting in a chair, looking at Carlos's back. Carlos was looking out of the window.

CHAPTER 22

L OUISE SAW CARLOS'S shoulders tense at her voice. Jamal jumped up and touched her arm.

"Listen, Lou..." Jamal started. Louise cut him off.

"What is he doing here?" Jamal flinched at the harshness in her voice.

"That's what I'm trying to explain. We talked. And I think you should talk to him." Jamal whispered.

"This? From you? I thought you were on my side."

"I'm still on your side. But you owe it to yourself to talk to him." Jamal squeezed her arm and walked out of the room, closing the door. Carlos still had his back to her. Louise looked at her phone. Harper texted her.

> **HARPER:** Talk to him, Lou.

So, everyone was in on this surprise. Louise let out a sigh.

"Harper, I get, but how did you convince Jamal?" she finally asked. Carlos didn't turn around.

"I texted him a lot yesterday. He didn't block me, like some people." Louise rolled her eyes. Carlos crossed his arms. Louise still stared at his back. She could hold on to her anger if she didn't look into his eyes.

"You lied to me. I wasn't ready to talk to you."

"Are you ready to talk to me now?"

"I don't feel like I have a choice."

"Jamal and Harper said that coming here would be a good idea. But if you don't want to talk to me, it's better if I leave."

Carlos finally turned around and looked at Louise. Her insides melted as she knew they would. His eyes were sad. She caused that sadness, and she wanted to rekindle the glow again. She turned her head away quickly. The tears welled up again. She closed her eyes. Why did she still hurt?

Carlos grasped her hand, then leaned his head on her. Louise knew she should pull away, but she didn't. Her heart was back in control now.

"Do you want me to leave?" He asked with the emotion deepening his voice. She could only shake her head in response. They stood like that for minutes as a few tears slipped from Louise's eyes.

"I'm still mad at you." She said, sounding like a child to herself.

"I'm so sorry, Louise. I would do anything to take it all back." Carlos pulled Louise into his chest. He murmured "I'm sorry" into her hair a few more times. Louise's hands were on his chest. She felt at home here in his arms, but she pushed back from him. She stared at his chest while she spoke.

"I don't know if I can forgive you yet. I can't handle lies. You betrayed me. But it's also not fair to put the pressure on you. We aren't even…"

Carlos put her hand over his heart. "You are my everything. I should have told you the first moment it became true. Louise, I'm falling in love with you."

She stiffened. She looked into his eyes and could see the truth in his words. It's only been a few weeks. They couldn't possibly be talking about love yet. She tried to step back, but he didn't let her go.

"I know this may be too fast for you and that is ok. I had to let you know in case you want me to leave. I shouldn't have lied to you. My job isn't worth the pain I caused you. I will forever be sorry for the lie, but I'm sorrier for what it did. I'm sorry I hurt you."

Another tear fell and Carlos wiped it from her cheek. She stepped back into him, burying her face in his chest. Louise couldn't look at him. She needed time to think, but everything he said overwhelmed her. She should tell him to leave her alone for a while so she can think without interruption.

"When do you have to leave?" She spoke into his shirt.

"My plane leaves in the morning." Louise nodded.

"Can I have a minute? I need to think about this." She looked up at his face. He looked pained. "You don't have to leave the house. I need to think. You overwhelm me."

Louise saw a small smile touch the side of Carlos's mouth. He let go of her and stepped back.

"I'll be right in there."

"I can smell the food, grab something to eat. We'll talk in a while."

He walked out the door and closed it behind him. Louise immediately felt the loss of his presence. She had to regain control of her emotions. She couldn't already be missing him. She sat in Jamal's chair and took a few deep breaths. Carlos told her he was falling in love with her. She didn't wake up this morning expecting to hear that. She needed to deal with him still being in town; love is not something she could deal with yet. Yesterday, she walked out of his life expecting to never see him again. But today...

Louise sank back into the chair. She had to decide if she wanted him gone or not. He already decided. He was here for her. Carlos hadn't given up on her. She had to decide if she would give up on him. The anger she felt when she first found out about his lie had lessened. She was still mad, but not at the level of anger and hurt from her last relationship. Thinking about that helped to put Carlos's deceit into perspective. He lied. It was, for a reason, a stupid reason. Louise knew what it was like to be consumed with your job. She was married to the Cummings. Her life revolved around running the estate. She made the choice to make the Cummings as her priority. So, she couldn't be too mad at Carlos for putting his job as a priority over whatever they were doing. It still hurt, though.

Louise had to be ready to forgive him. At least that will help her let the pain go. With the pain gone, the question becomes, did she want to try a relationship with Carlos? The answer to that was still yes. Knowing that a long-distance relationship would fail, she still wanted to try with him. Why was she still in this room when Carlos was on the other side of the door?

She heard a soft knock. She beamed. Carlos must have had the same thought. She told him to come in. It was Angie. She had a plate of food in her hand.

"We thought you must be hungry by now." Louise looked at her phone. She had been in the room for an hour thinking. Angie placed the plate on the table and sat in the other chair. "You want to talk?"

Louise shook her head.

"Well, here eat. They are on pins and needles, waiting for you. Silas and I flipped a coin to see who would come and check on you. Jay and Harp think you are mad at them. Are you?"

"A little. They shouldn't have gone behind my back," Louise replied.

"Would you have come if you knew he was here?" Angie asked.

"No, but they still should have told me." Louise waited a minute before she could say her next words.

"He's falling in love with me." Louise said it to Angie to get her friend's reaction. Angie nodded.

"That reads about right. Are you falling in love with him? Cause if you aren't, it's time to cut him loose," admonished Angie.

"That is harsh!" Louise shot back.

"True, but it's better than having him hopeful and hanging on. He is a good guy, Lou. If you can't forgive him for lying to you, then let him work on getting over you."

Louise stood. She grabbed the plate and headed to the door. She took a deep breath and opened it. Everyone else was sitting around the dining table. They all looked at her as she entered the space. This moment reminded her why she hated an open floor plan. There was an open chair next to Carlos. She went to it, sat, and began eating her food.

"That's all we get?" Jamal asked. She looked at him, then rolled her eyes. She reached for Carlos's hand and held it.

"I'm not talking to you two right now." She pointed to Jamal, then Harper, a smile forming on her face. "Silas, the food is excellent."

She felt Carlos squeeze her hand. She looked at him and smiled fully. He looked back, finally showing her the smile she loved. He reached over and took her face and his hands. The question was in his eyes. She leaned into him, and they kissed.

"Ok, Jay, looks like we lost the cutest couple award," Silas said. Louise laughed into Carlos's mouth and pulled back.

"We still have a lot to talk about, but I'll accept the cutest couple award." Louise said.

A YEAR LATER

L OUISE RUSHED THROUGH her morning routine. She wanted to get to the estate as soon as possible. She decided against her usual work outfit for her brand-new sweater. It was forest green with gold and silver trees all over it. She put on a pair of jeans and silver boots. She completed the look with silver Christmas tree earrings and a gold reindeer headband. She grabbed her coat and ran up to the estate.

When she entered the doors, she looked up to the ceiling before looking at his chair. Carlos was sitting there smiling her smile. She opened her coat, and he looked at her sweater appreciatively. She walked over to him. He pulled her into his lap and kissed her.

"Is that what you have been hiding from me?"

"Yes. I can't believe you snuck out before me. Why didn't I hear an alarm?"

"I didn't set one. I was too excited to sleep, anyway."

Later in the day, Carlos's family would be in town to visit the estate for the first time. Louise had already met them, so she wasn't nervous about that. She wanted them to fall in love with the estate as much as Carlos had.

"Well, we have a very busy morning, Mr. Hernández, so you better perk up." Louise stood up and took Carlos's hand to pull him up.

"Whatever you say, Ms. Cummings." They walked hand in hand to her office.

Carlos quit his job the day he got back to L.A. It was more of a mutual decision. After Malcolm stopped his sale of the shares, Carlos admitted to his management team that he helped encourage Malcolm against selling. Louise was happy for Carlos, as he seemed to be happier away from the job. She also was happy because he booked a one-way ticket and stayed at the estate for a month. They could get to know each other better. In their conversations, Carlos realized he enjoyed consulting for the clients through his old company. He opened his own consulting firm to help businesses grow. The Cummings Estate was his first client.

He officially moved to Sacamore that summer. The quickness of their romance still shocked Louise. Six months after meeting Carlos, she was living with him. Tomorrow would be the anniversary of the day she met him. But before they could celebrate, they had to get through the final decorations of the estate. She wanted everything to be perfect for his nieces and nephew. They didn't get to see the theme for last year, so this year she wanted it to be magical for them.

The theme for this year's decoration was Toyland. Louise had a ball picking out toys, games, and stuff animals to put around the estate. They would decorate the back of the estate like a life-sized Candyland game, with the tree being the main event. It excited Louise that they would out-do last year's theme.

As they worked in her office that morning, Louise had a smile on her face. Carlos was sitting in his chair, a place he still spent most of his time, even though Louise gave him an office to work in. She looked at his curls. He kept his hair longer after she told him she loves running her fingers through those curls.

"I don't seem to get anything done with you around." He said with a smirk.

"You have an entire office you could be in right now."

"Can I do this from that office?" He reached out and grasped her hand.

"How is it going? Did you secure the client?"

His 100-watt smile brightened his face. "Yes, I sent over the contract. Looks like I'll be in Reno next year. And this is a small boutique hotel. They are looking to expand. I'll be gone for a few weeks in January."

"I'm so happy for you. You are excited about Nevada, aren't you?"

"I'm still a 'sunshine person'! Last January was so cold. But I will miss you every second."

"I believe you will miss me, but you also have the biggest smile on your face." She laughed.

"True." Before Louise could mess with Carlos anymore about his trip, she got a message from Harper. Louise opened her phone and looked at the text.

> **HARPER:** I did a stupid thing. I don't know what to do.

> **LOUISE:** What's up? It couldn't have been that bad.

> **ANGIE:** What is going on?

> **HARPER:** I slept with Mack last night!

Louise dropped her phone on her desk. Mack has been friends with the three of them their whole lives. He had been in love with Harper about the same time. Harper never gave him a chance, and he stopped trying when they were all in high school. Louise knew this revelation would cause another interesting holiday.

"What's wrong?" Carlos asked. Louise couldn't respond to him.

> **ANGIE:** What?!

> **HARPER:** I know. I need help.

> **LOUISE:** How can we help you? You already did it!

> **HARPER:** I'm hiding out in his bathroom. What should I do? How can I get out?

> **ANGIE:** That sure is a different Christmas gift you are giving him this year. Can you sneak out the window?

> **HARPER:** Angie, I don't need jokes right now. I think the window is big enough.

> **LOUISE:** Ang! Why are we considering this? She needs to put on her big girl panties…do you even have any?

> **HARPER:** Louise…

> **LOUISE:** Sorry, walk out the front door like a normal person. Tell him goodbye. What does this mean, anyway? Are you two together?

> **HARPER:** Lou! No! What is wrong with me? Ok, I'm going out.

Loise looked up from her phone at Carlos.

"Is everything alright?" He asked.

"I don't think so. I know that it's going to be another dramatic holiday."

HARPER

SHOOT, SHOOT, SHOOT! What is wrong with me? Ok, Louise is right. I'll walk out there and say I had a great time and leave. Thank goodness I drove myself out here. Why did I drive myself out here? I should've texted Lou and Ang. Lou would have let me come by the house. What is wrong with me? Anyone but Mack. Ok, I'm going to walk out there, say goodbye and walk out the front door. Is he cooking? Oh no! I smell eggs. He is making me breakfast.

Harper banged her head against the bathroom door. She was already dressed but needed her shoes and coat to leave. She looked in the mirror. Her hair was a curly mess, and she had nothing to tie it up. Last week, she colored it a dark green color, so today it looked like a forest. Her skin glowed from a wonderful night with the wrong person. She was used to that happening. She spent many nights with many wrong people, but this one was worse. She couldn't believe she had sex with one of her best friends. She's known Mack since she was five years old. He was the first boy she pushed over in kindergarten. He told her many times that was the moment he realized he would marry her.

Why Mack? Of all people? Harper took a deep breath and walked out of the bathroom. Mack was in his kitchen stirring something in a pan. His back was to her. It was a broad back. He was taller than her by many inches and had rich, dark skin. He turned to her and had a brilliant smile on his face. His locks hung around his face and his shirt was open, showing off his amazing physique and eight-pack abs. His being shirtless showed how much time he spent outdoors. He had a long beard that she had stroked the night before. She was a sucker for a well-groomed beard. She shook her head. She had to keep those thoughts out of her head. He walked towards her, his smile change to something sultrier.

Harper backed up and started looking for her shoes.

"Harp, is something wrong?"

"No, I need to find my shoes."

"They are by the door."

Harper went to the door and put them on. She grabbed her coat and turned to Mack.

"I had a good time last night. Thanks." Harper unlocked the door and opened it partially. She turned again to Mack. His face had fallen. Her heart twisted. She walked out the door, knowing that she had broken her best friend's heart.

Harper's story will continue July 2023.

ACKNOWLEDGEMENTS

I made the decision to be a writer before I knew what that meant. I thought it meant to write a story then bam, a book. Little girl me was so cute. No! It takes a team and a force of will to create a book.

I'd like to thank my editor, Ronei Harden. She helped me get through my overuse of words to get to a story that others will understand.

I like to thank the team at Alt 19 Creative for creating the perfect cover for my story. The Cummings Estate is its own character and they captured it perfectly. Also, making this book real, both physically and digitally.

To the writers that have held me up during this process, a special thank you. I have had the best writing groups! First the Painted Steps writing group. We started off as a group of 6 then whittled down to Jolandi, Lee, Tom, and me. I felt at times so intimidated, but you all always made me feel like I could be a "real" writer. An Author. We were a group spread out across the world and ages, but we made magic. That book will get published one day! Second, the Aspiring Writers Association of America (AWAOA). This group has been so encouraging, loving, and supportive. If it wasn't for AWAOA, I wouldn't have published my first short story. I became a real published author. That was the step I needed to show me that I could do this, I could have a real book with my (pen) name on it.

To the best writing mentor on earth (I'm bias and I don't care) Andi Floyd, Thank, thank you! To know that the classes I took from you almost ten years ago (and me not doing my homework a lot), would lead me here. Wow! Thank you for getting me this far and to the next level and more.

I have the best friends a girl could wish for. They support, love, listen and talk me down from giving up constantly. If you don't have friends like that, get some.

My Mama started this whole thing. She had a curious kid that loved stories that she had to constantly read too. That kid got bored by the same old stories, so she made up stories on a nightly basis to please that kid. Well, Mama, those stories worked. Now it's time for you to share your stories with the world. (And they are good because I used to sneak and read them!)

If you made it this far, I want to let you know that if I can do it, you can do it too. I'm just a regular person with a story to tell. We all have stories.

ABOUT THE AUTHOR

Brigitte Carter is a hopeful romantic that never gives up on love no matter how hard it can be. She has tried and failed but will try again at love. For now, she is happy to share her stories of love and misunderstandings and that hilarity that comes when two people decide to give each other a chance.

You will find her wrapped up in a good book (or a good man), in her kitchen baking or out enjoying the sun.

Connect with her at www.BrigitteCarterAuthor.com
or scan the QR code: